Crane wrapped ... mising himself he wo... g ever hurt her.

He rubbed her back, feeling her leanness, her toughness, and her softness.

"Everything will be fine," he murmured.

No sooner had he spoken the words than he wished for them back. He couldn't be making promises he didn't know if he could keep. The feel of her in his arms had turned his mind to mush.

He cupped a hand over her hair. It was so silky. Like nothing he could remember feeling before. He lowered his head, letting his lips caress her hair. He was drowning in the scent of her, the feel of her, the pound of his heart against her slight form.

"God took care of us today," she murmured, her voice muffled against his chest.

Her breath was sweet and tempting, and he lowered his head a fraction more, willing her to lift her face and offer her lips.

Instead she pushed away.

LINDA FORD draws on her own experiences living in the Canadian prairie and Rockies to paint wonderful adventures in romance and faith. She lives in Alberta, Canada, with her family, writing as much as her full-time job of taking care of a paraplegic and four kids who are still at home will allow. Linda says, "I thank God that he has given me a full productive life and that I'm not bored. I thank Him for placing a little bit of the creative energy revealed in his creation into me, and I pray I might use my writing for his honor and glory."

HEARTSONG PRESENTS

Books by Linda Ford
HP240—The Sun Still Shines
HP268—Unchained Hearts
HP368—The Heart Seeks a Home
HP448—Chastity's Angel

Crane's
Bride

Linda Ford

Heartsong Presents

To my husband, Ivan:
Together we have journeyed many years,
faced many hardships, enjoyed many adventures,
and grown together in love.

A note from the author:
I love to hear from my readers! You may correspond with me
by writing: **Linda Ford**
Author Relations
PO Box 719
Uhrichsville, OH 44683

ISBN 1-58660-474-0

CRANE'S BRIDE

All Scripture quotations are taken from the King James Version of
the Bible.

All of the characters and events in this book are fictitious. Any
resemblance to actual persons, living or dead, or to actual events
is purely coincidental.

Cover illustration by Greg Roman.

PRINTED IN THE U.S.A.

one

Crane had figured out everything else before he headed west. The farther west he went, the more the neglected detail bothered him.

He leaned forward in his saddle and stared at the town ahead, a fair-to-middling-sized place, looking as if it had sprung helter-skelter from the land with half-finished buildings and a wide dirt street.

"Ain't much," he muttered to the ever-patient Rebel.

The horse tossed his head. Town meant a warm stall and a good grooming, and he sidestepped in an effort to get his rider moving.

"Ain't much," Crane repeated. "But it ain't going to get any better." Towns were meaner and farther apart with every passing day.

He pushed his dusty cowboy hat back from his forehead and scratched his head. "About time for a bath." And to take care of this other business plaguing his thoughts ever since he'd made up his mind what he was going to do.

"Let's go." He flicked the reins and tugged the lead rope of the packhorse. He pulled in under the sign "Colhome General Store," turning his back on the curious stares of the two old codgers who lounged on the wooden chairs. They were watching him as he secured both horses to the rail.

Crane wiped his palms along his thighs and stepped to the lean-to veranda. One old coot spat on the boards close to Crane's boots. Crane drew to a halt, glaring at the old man until he wiped his grizzled mouth and turned away.

Inside, Crane paused for his eyes to adjust to the dim light, then ran his gaze over the store interior. Nothing but the usual dusty shelves and two old women fingering some yard goods. The rail-thin storekeep studied Crane over the top of his wire glasses, as if examining some rare and unwelcome bug. Crane fixed him with a steady narrow-eyed look, forcing the man to lower his gaze.

His boots thudded on the oiled boards as he crossed to the counter. "I want to put up a notice." His lazy drawl gave no hint of the way his insides were knotted up, as if he were scared.

Only he wasn't scared. He'd thought on this and knew exactly what he was doing. Besides, near as he could figure, there was no other way.

"Go ahead." The storekeeper jerked a thumb toward the pocked board and busied himself with a handful of bills.

"Got a piece of paper?"

"Sure. Cost you a penny."

Crane dug a coin from his pocket and flicked it to the counter. The man swept it into his palm and drew a square of paper from under the stained boards, then turned back to his bills. Crane waited, scowling at the top of the man's head. "Can I borrow a pencil?"

"Sure thing." He offered a pencil stub on the tip of stained fingers. "No charge."

Crane licked the lead and carefully wrote the message he'd composed. Finished, he pulled a jackknife from his pocket, dug out a tack, and put up his notice.

The storekeep stretched his neck like a chicken so he could see Crane's note. He mouthed the words, then glared at Crane.

Crane cared little what the man thought. He retreated to the nails and saws, pretending to examine the merchandise.

"Can I help you?" The bespectacled man watched his every move.

"I'll let you know." He edged around so he could see the door.

A gray-haired matron bustled in, conducted her business, and left. One of the old codgers from the veranda shuffled to the door, peered in, then returned to his post. Two schoolgirls came in, whispering and giggling, selected two cents' worth of candy, and giggled their way out.

Crane waited, ignoring the looks he got. His stomach rumbled.

He'd about decided to come back later when the door opened and another lady hustled in. Crane squinted, but against the bright window he couldn't determine whether she was young or old, ugly or otherwise. All he could say for certain was that she was reed thin, wore a dark dress, and moved as if she were in a hurry. He tensed and drew in his breath.

The girl, or woman if she was that, rushed to the counter, bent over it to make a low-spoken request, then turned as the storekeep chose an item from behind the counter. The girl checked the room in a sweeping glance and, with nothing to detain her interest, studied the notice board, bending forward as she saw Crane's notice.

Crane began to sweat. His stomach had been kissing his backbone for a spell and now groaned so loud he was sure it could be heard across the room.

She tore the notice from the board and shoved it toward the storekeep. "You know who put this up?"

The man behind the counter jerked his head toward Crane. She whirled to face him. He wished he could see her better, but before he could figure a way, she marched across the floor, her steps crisp and quick.

"You the man who wrote this?" She shook the note in his face.

She's not very big. In fact, she looks as if a stiff wind will blow her away. His mind whirled without lighting on another thought. Again his stomach growled. "Yup," he managed through the confusion of his thoughts.

She studied him from head to toe, taking her time about it.

He wondered what she saw. A dusty cowboy, lean and tough as shoe leather? Another saddle bum with too-long blond hair darkened by days in the saddle?

Suddenly his arms felt too long, and he crossed them over

his chest. Her gaze lingered on his boots. He followed her stare, wishing he'd taken time to remove the evidence of the last trail ride.

She jerked her head up and boldly met his eyes.

He braced himself.

"I'm a God-fearing woman. I'll be your wife." Never once did she blink.

His thoughts exploded. He didn't know what he'd expected. Nor could he explain why he'd worded the notice the way he did, but something inside insisted she must be God-fearing. Her gaze bore into his until he clenched his jaw. Her look demanded an answer, and he croaked, "Yup."

Her brow puckered, and she glanced at the note in her hand. "You write this yourself?"

"Yup." His mind spun like the wheel on a runaway buggy. Now would be a good time to find the back door and use it, but her eyes riveted him to the spot. The light caught in her hair. Black, he thought. Black and shiny.

"Then I guess you can read and write. But can you talk?"

Beads of sweat collected on Crane's forehead. He managed another "Yup." At the sound of his own voice, thick and slow, his brain slammed its fist. He grabbed her elbow. "Let's get out of here."

There was no resistance in her arm as they hustled from the store. Outside, desperate for a retreat from the prying eyes following his every move, he turned in the direction of the river. Despite her shortness, the girl had no trouble keeping up with his hurried strides. He liked that, he decided.

Neither of them slowed until they ducked through the sprawling willows and faced the tumbling river. He dropped his hold on her arm and stared at the sparkling water.

"I'm headed west. Going to start a new life. I need a woman—a wife." He'd said it badly, but the fine words he'd practiced for three days had fled.

"Fine. I'm willing."

He looked at this woman who had agreed to marry him.

He could see over her head without a hair in his view. Small, he thought again. And thin. He narrowed his eyes. She looked downright starved. But he liked the way the light caught in her hair, trapped in the black strands.

He met her eyes then. Blue as ink and unblinking. Full of defiant challenge. Even the way she stood, hands clenched at her side, feet gripping the ground, spoke a warning. He couldn't help but admire her spunk.

As he studied her more closely, he wondered if he'd made a dumb move. He had no desire to get hitched to a dirty woman, and this was one of the dirtiest he'd seen. Although her hair had been brushed smooth and tied at her neck, her dress was ragged and soiled, and—he wrinkled his nose— she desperately needed a bath. Her eyes narrowed as if reading his mind, and again her gaze traveled his length as if to remind him of his own condition.

"I meant to have a bath as soon as I hit town," he said.

She nodded. "I'm dirty, and I know it. Don't need no reminding. The dirt will come off with a dip in the river, but I won't pretend I'm something I'm not. This dress is all I got." Her eyes amazed him. Never once shifting away from his, they darkened, and he saw—no, he felt—her pride like a fist driven into his chest.

Pushing his hat back, he rubbed his forehead. Clothes and bathing were easy to solve, but other things needed to be sorted out. "First things first," he murmured.

She nodded.

"Are you running away?" All he needed was an angry father or husband barking at his heels.

Her jaw tightened. "Not running away—running to."

"And what would you be meaning by that?"

"Same as you. I'm looking for a new life."

"I'm not promising you anything but a home, a fair share of whatever I have, and probably lots of hard work." He'd struggled for three days for a way to say this, to make plain what he wanted and at the same time let her know what he did not expect. He did not expect love or passion, only a wife and a home to complete his new life.

"You trying to say this is to be a businesslike arrangement?" Her clear voice was brittle.

He nodded.

"You're wanting to make sure I'm not expecting romance?"

He grimaced at the way she spat it out but silently thanked her for putting words to his thoughts. "I'm looking for a partner for my new life, nothing more."

Her blue eyes flashing, she drew herself straighter and fixed him with a hard look. "Fine. I'm willing to work, and I don't need much. There's only one thing."

He raised his eyebrows and waited.

Her scowl was dark. "You ever hit me and I'm gone."

Crane jerked back at the thought. He wasn't a fool. He knew some men figured women were no better than a cow or a dog, but he had been raised differently. His frail mother would have dissolved at his feet if he'd even raised his voice in anger.

He studied the creature glowering at him and decided she could hardly be considered frail despite her small size. She had the bearing and boldness of a born fighter, and he wanted to know more about her.

"I will never hit you," he promised, but her shoulders remained hunched. "And if I ever do, you can leave without any questions asked."

Slowly she relaxed, and Crane let his breath out. Again they studied each other.

"My name's Crane." He held out his hand.

She hesitated, then grasped it and gave a quick shake. "I'm Maggie."

Her hand was very small, yet her grip firm.

"We'll go back to the store and get enough for the coming months." He felt her shift in emotions even before he saw her eyes darken with what he figured must be acceptance, even anticipation. "We're both needing a bath. We'll go to the hotel and shed ourselves of this dirt."

"I'd as soon bathe in the river," she announced.

He searched her eyes for a clue to her meaning, but she continued to stare at him fiercely.

Finally he shrugged. "Suit yourself. Now let's get fixed up." He strode in the direction of town, leaving Maggie to follow at his heels.

They proceeded directly to the store. The uncooperative storekeep's attitude changed quick as a wink when he saw the coins Crane clinked to the counter. "We'll be needing a few things," Crane muttered, his gaze following Maggie as she plucked two dresses from the ready-made rack. He'd instructed her to buy all she would need without regard for cost. "No telling what we'll find ahead of us." Within minutes she had gathered a number of items, hesitating before she added a cake of soap and a length of toweling.

He would have preferred to lie back in a tub of hot water, but he followed her back to the river, leading the horses and carrying the bundle from the store. With a murmured explanation, she pointed toward a canopy of overhanging willows. Crane nodded and followed the river in the opposite direction until he found another secluded spot.

The water was still icy from the spring thaw. Crane lathered up quickly, then held his breath as he plunged under the surface, shaking his head and shuddering as he emerged. The brisk rubdown restored but a fraction of the heat he'd lost in his dip. Running a comb through his hair, he wondered if he had time for a barbershop cut and as quickly dismissed the idea. He wanted only one thing, and that was to get this done with and get back on the trail.

He waited for Maggie to reappear. When she pushed aside the willows, his mouth fell open, and he stared. *She cleans up real nice.* Her scrubbed skin held the pink glow of a sunset.

"You look good," he murmured, amazed when the pink in her cheeks deepened, and he understood it was because of what he said.

"You too," she said.

He shuffled as warmth crept up his neck and hoped his cheeks didn't darken in the same telltale way.

They retraced their steps to the heart of town and a low building offering food.

"I bringee man big breakfast?" offered the waiter of uncertain origins.

"What would you be wanting, Maggie?"

Maggie perched on the edge of the chair, her glance darting about the room. Crane knew the moment she'd checked every person and knew too she had been looking for something or someone. Finding them absent, she filled her lungs and relaxed. "The same."

After days of campfire cooking and gulping from a tin cup, Crane savored the hot coffee served in heavy white china. His concentration eliminated the need for conversation yet gave him a chance to study his soon-to-be bride, suddenly struck by how young she looked.

"How old are you?" He had no intention of playing her nursemaid.

"Eighteen." Again that blue-eyed directness. "But I know how to work and take care of myself if that's what's bothering you. How old are you?" She drummed her fingers on the table.

He had to think. "Twenty-seven, near as I can recall." He chuckled. "And I know how to work and take care of myself."

She blinked, then laughed, low and musical. Her blue eyes sparkled with splinters of light. Crane stared like an idiot.

Heaping plates of steak, eggs, fried potatoes, and flapjacks were set before them. Crane dug into the food without a second look. By the time he cleaned his plate, he knew he'd enjoyed a hearty breakfast and figured Maggie would surely be stalled by now, but she steadily plowed through the mound, finishing up shortly after he did.

"You ate the whole thing."

Her cheeks bloomed pink. "I was hungry."

"I guess so." If she ate like that every day, he would spend all his time foraging food.

"I haven't eaten in three days," she whispered. "Since I walked away from—" She didn't finish.

He rubbed his forehead. "You better explain yourself."

"It's not what you think." She took a deep breath. "I was working at the hotel in exchange for a place to sleep and some food." Her fingers twisted around each other. "My job was to clean up rooms after the guests." She shuddered, and Crane could only guess at the things she'd done.

"When the hotel owner wanted me to do other things"—her eyes grew stormy—"I left." She squirmed forward until she balanced on the edge of the chair.

Finally he nodded. "And you left everything you own."

She shrugged. "It weren't much."

Seems like what he had to offer, no matter how slim, was an improvement. He felt rather pleased with himself. He pushed his chair back, and she sprang up, bouncing on the balls of her feet. He clamped his hat on, and they ambled toward the livery barn, where Crane ran his practiced gaze over the available mounts, choosing a well-built mare for Maggie.

She slid her hands along the mare's neck and whispered to the animal in a way that assured Crane she was at ease with the horse. "I shall call her Liberty."

The significance of her choice was not lost on Crane, and he smiled, hoping they would both find what they wanted in their new life—sweet liberty for her and, for him, help in building a home. A vague yearning tugged at his thoughts, but it disappeared as swiftly as it came, and he had not the time or patience to search after it.

They repacked the animals, Maggie working alongside Crane with a quiet quickness he found comforting. Then they headed toward the little church where the man who sold them the horse said they would find a preacher.

With every step, Crane's resolve strengthened. It was what he had decided to do; Maggie seemed pleasant enough and, now that she was cleaned up, not hard on the eyes. Whatever there was to discover about each other, they would have plenty of time to find it out on the trail.

And so he stood before the preacher with Maggie at his side.

"Do you Byler Thomas Crane take Margaret Malone to be your lawful wedded wife?"

He answered, "I do."

The short ceremony ended, and they stepped outside into the bright afternoon sun. "Well, Mrs. Crane, are you ready to set out?" He grinned down at her.

She nodded, keeping her head bent. "The sooner the better."

In order to pick up the trail to the west, they traversed several streets, dirtier with each step, the buildings increasingly ugly. The whole place smelled of trouble, and Crane kept sharp attention.

As they drew abreast of a narrow alleyway, he heard a high-pitched scream followed by gasping fear-laced wails, then a sudden flash of pink and white to his right.

A child. The small body rocketed across his path, with thundering steps in pursuit. Crane had his hands full, holding Rebel, who snorted and reared.

Out of the corner of his eye, he saw Maggie drop to the ground and wondered if she had been thrown, but he was too busy with Rebel to offer help. As soon as he'd calmed his horse, he dismounted, searching for the figure he was sure had been battered by Rebel's hooves, but a man scooped up the small child.

"Let me go!" the child shrieked. "I won't go back!"

Crane saw it all in a heartbeat. The swelling arms of a blacksmith tightening around the tiny body clad only in skimpy white undergarments. The anger darkening his face. Crane clenched his fists at his side. He was no match for this bulk of a man, and it was none of his business, but his gut wrenched.

A figure in a blue-flowered dress he recognized as being one he'd purchased just a few hours earlier skidded to a halt in front of the struggling pair. Maggie planted herself in the man's path, her hands on her hips. "This your child?"

"He ain't my father. He ain't nothing." The child's sobs

tore at Crane's mind like a cold winter gale.

"Get out of my way." The burly man pushed Maggie aside with a thick arm.

She swayed but held her ground.

Cold steel filled Crane, and he stepped toward them with casual deliberateness.

"Put her down," Maggie growled, her fists clenching and unclenching at her side.

"Lady, you best mind yer own bizness." He lifted his hand.

Crane pushed the hand away, at the same time shoving Maggie behind him. "What seems to be the problem?" He balanced on the balls of his feet, his words low and lazy.

"No problem." The burly man dropped his arm. "Just claiming what's rightfully mine."

"Put her down." Maggie again faced the man.

A gleam jerked at Crane's nerves, and he stared at his Colt .45 gripped in her hands.

"Where'd you get that?" Something akin to knifepoints scraped along his nerves.

She didn't answer, but there was no need. He'd hung the revolver on the pack animal. He was not a fighting man, but neither was he naive as to the need for a gun.

"Maggie, what do you think you're up to?"

"I'm doing what any decent person would do," she answered without shifting her gaze. Again she ordered the man, "Let that child go."

With a volley of curses, the man lunged at Maggie. She neatly sidestepped and fired.

Dust at the man's feet kicked up, and Crane saw a hole in the toe of his boot. His muscles coiled to spring. "Why you—"

"Let her go, or I'll shoot you." She jerked away as he swung a fist at her.

She fired another shot, removing his hat. He gingerly rubbed his head.

The child squirmed from his grasp, skidding out of reach of the three adults, her glance darting from one to the other.

Crane had seen that hunted look in wild animals. The child seemed not far removed from a wild animal with her matted hair and scruffy appearance.

"Honey, who is this man, and what does he want with you?" Maggie kept the gun trained on the man as she addressed the child.

The child shook like leaves before a wind. "He thinks he owns me 'cause I don't have no folks."

"That so, Mister?" The voice, so sweet and gentle when speaking to the child, carried a hard, warning note.

Crane smiled at the contrast.

"She's mine. I owned her mother, and I own her." He jerked his head down the alley. At the end of the lane, Crane saw a mean building and knew it for what it was—a place of disrepute. He shuddered to think of anyone, least of all a child, having to live there. *You don't own people. Nobody can own another.*

"You got any papers to prove that?" Maggie pressed the man.

He spat. "Don't need any. Nobody gonna argue about it." He spat again, his spittle landing at Maggie's feet.

A small crowd had assembled, and their mute silence proved his words.

"Nobody but me," Maggie snarled, turning to the child. "You want to come with us?"

Her eyes bright, the child nodded.

Unmindful of Maggie's gun, the man roared and reached for the quaking child.

Quicksilver-like, Maggie grabbed her and, in a swift movement, sprang for her horse, lifting the child behind the saddle and jumping up in front of her.

"Let's go!" Maggie called.

Crane didn't have time to think about who was right. "Ride!" he called, but he could have saved his breath. She was already leaning over the neck of her horse, urging it forward. They raced toward the open trail. Shots rang out behind them, and Crane ducked lower.

two

Crane narrowed his eyes, forcing them to focus on bits of the racing landscape to examine them for danger. He saw speeding trees and one lone shack—the only visible occupant a brown-speckled hen, flapping and squawking a protest at the clattering trio.

The only other sounds were pounding hooves and the heaving breath of his horse. The flying mane stung Crane's cheeks as he kept his head low to avoid any bullets aimed at them, but he heard no more. His thoughts galloped at a pace every bit as swift as their flight. *All I wanted was someone to help set up a home in the new West.*

The last few minutes were giving him pause for thought. Not in his wildest dreams had he considered he might be biting off more than he could chew.

He kept at a gallop until they crested a hill some miles from town, where he slowed Rebel, turning him to face the back trail. For several minutes he squinted toward town, now a low cluster in the distance. Maggie pulled up beside him.

"I don't see nobody after us."

Crane held his peace, willing their dust to settle so he could be certain.

Maggie stood in her stirrups and shaded her eyes. "You see something?"

Finally he eased back and lifted his hat to let the breeze sift through his hair. "Don't see nothing. Don't necessarily mean there ain't nothing." But they'd had plenty of time to mount a party to ride after them. Perhaps the townspeople had refused to help the burly man. Maybe they'd decided one little bitty child wasn't worth the effort.

Maggie murmured to the mare as it pranced nervously and

17

settled again, half a head in front of Rebel, allowing Crane to study Maggie without turning his head. She clutched the child's arm around her waist. Her skirt flowed around her legs. She strained forward, still watching for pursuers. Every muscle seemed taut, every nerve alert, yet he sensed no fear.

A suspicion grew. He could have sworn she was enjoying this inordinately much, and again he wondered what he had gotten himself into. He slapped his hat to his head, pulling it low. "Let's go." He paused, his gaze fixed to the front. "We'll put some space between us and them. Then we'll talk." He looked squarely at Maggie and the child. These were not saddle-hardened men at his side. "You both up to this?"

Maggie's eyes snapped. "We certainly are." She dipped her head to the child. "Aren't we?"

Eyes wide, the child glanced at Crane, turning away quickly, her whispered yes barely audible.

They kept a steady pace for another hour or more, riding in silence. Crane wondered if Maggie's thoughts were as confused as his; as for the child, he had no notion what such a little thing would be thinking.

The sun had passed its hiatus when Crane reined in. "There's a good spot over there. We'll give the horses a break." He wasn't going to invite any more surprises, and he led the way to a thick grove of trees close to the river. They could water the horses and still be able to see the trail.

Maggie swung down, pulling the child after her, then stiffly turned her horse to water. Crane did the same, taking his time. It wasn't until the horses had been led to a grassy spot and left to graze that he faced Maggie.

"Do you mind telling me what you think we're going to do now?" His voice was low.

She shuffled her feet in the sand.

Crane waited, his gaze lazily resting on the top of her head. Could be she was regretting her haste.

She snapped her head up so suddenly he jerked back. "What else could I do?" Her eyes flashed.

"Besides shoot the man dead, you mean?" Perhaps he should count himself lucky she hadn't. "Where did you learn to shoot like that?"

She grinned. "A boy taught me."

He held up his hand. "I don't want to know. Next thing you'll be telling me you're part of a gang of bank robbers."

She laughed, a sound echoing the bubbling water behind him. "It wasn't near that exciting. I was about twelve or thirteen, and a neighbor boy begged his dad to teach him to shoot. His dad gave him an old pistol and told him to go practice." She shrugged. "I tagged along."

"I can't say whether or not it was good you did. Seems like it's given you call to get yourself into a heap of trouble."

She looked past him, a distant longing in her expression. Finally she turned her blue eyes toward him, direct and challenging. "What would you have me do?" She shivered. "It don't take any imagination to guess what kind of life she's had." Her eyes darkened. "And what's in store for her. Somebody needed to help her."

He couldn't argue that. "Why'd it have to be you?"

"You see anyone else rushing in?"

"No." He wanted to tell her the code of the West: Keep your nose out of other people's business. But her chin jutted out, and he was pretty sure she would have told him that was all well and good in most situations, but this wasn't one of them.

The child sat with her toes in the water, peeping out from under a curtain of tangled hair. Seeing him look at her, she ducked her head.

"What do you expect to do with her?"

"Why, I figured she would go west with us."

"How do you figure? You don't just ride into town, snatch a child, and ride away without so much as a 'do you mind' or 'if you please.'" Crane kept his voice low, disguising the tension stiffening his spine.

"A body shouldn't ignore a child in need, even if it means

stepping on toes." Her taut voice made Crane wonder why she cared so much. How little he knew about this woman who was now his wife. He had a wife! In all the excitement he'd almost forgotten. Not only a wife, but now a child as well.

He looked more closely at the child. "She ain't very big."

"Size means nothing." She spat the words out.

He guessed she meant something by that, but he wasn't about to go nosing down an unfamiliar trail.

She answered him even though he hadn't asked. "It's your heart that counts. How you look at things."

They stood side by side watching the child. He pushed his hat back. "She got a name?"

"I 'spect so. Everybody's got a name." She paused. "Sweetheart, come here."

The child slowly turned toward them, looking at the ground, her toes clenching in the sand. She studiously avoided eye contact with Crane.

He looked at her—really looked at her—for the first time. Big brown eyes, a mat of blond hair, a hunted look. "I don't know much about little ones."

Maggie motioned the child closer but directed her words at Crane. "You got no brothers and sisters?"

The little one inched toward them, her tiny limbs stiff. He could smell her fear. It made the skin on the back of his neck tingle. "No, I was the onliest one."

Maggie looked at him for a moment. "Huh," was all she said before turning back to the child, rocking back and forth just out of reach. "You got a name, Child?"

Big brown eyes stared unblinkingly at Maggie. "My mamma"—she swallowed hard—"my mamma done call me Betsy." Her words carried on the breeze.

Maggie nodded. "That sounds like a right nice name to me."

A trace of a smile transformed the child's face for a heartbeat.

"You got another name, a last name?" Maggie prodded.

The child shook her head. "I don't know. My mamma not tell me."

"That's fine," Maggie said as the child's fingers plucked at the material around her waist. "Betsy, do you know how old you are?"

"Maybe five. Maybe six." She twisted the material into a knot.

Maggie turned to Crane. "What's today's date?"

"I believe the preacher wrote May tenth, eighteen ninety."

"Look at that, Betsy. Your birthday and our wedding are on the same day."

Crane stared at the child's tiny fingers and pint-sized feet.

"Well, what you going to do with her?" Maggie's question jerked at his senses.

"Me? Seems this is your doing." His slow words hid his turmoil.

She flung her hands out. "You played a part too."

He watched the river gurgle by; he saw the trees whispering in the breeze. He could not think.

"You got to choose—either we take her with us, or you have to ride back to town and give her back to that horrible man." She spat out the last few words.

He blinked and turned on her. "Ride back there? Why me?" She sure had a funny notion of what was right for him.

"I'd go with you if you want."

He didn't want, and he had no intention of taking the child back, which left him few choices.

"Wash her up," he told Maggie. "I'll get a shirt for her. She can't ride around the country half naked."

Maggie looked at him open-mouthed. Then a slow grin spread across her face, and her eyes flashed bright blue before she led Betsy to the water's edge.

Crane stared after them. How had he managed to end up this far from where he was only this morning? With a shake of his head, he trudged toward the horses, rifling through his pack to pull out a faded denim shirt. He shook it, trying to imagine the child wearing it. His mental powers failed to produce any sort of image. He'd have to buy her some proper clothes at the next town. And shoes. You needed shoes to head west.

He grabbed the bar of soap and towel and returned to the river. Maggie stood beside Betsy in water to their ankles. Betsy. He turned the name over in his mind, trying to get used to the feel of it. The child shook enough to rattle her bones.

Maggie spoke to her, but Crane did not catch what she said. The child nodded, clutching her hands in the hem of her undershirt.

Maggie acknowledged Crane. "Good. You've brought the soap." She took bar and shirt. "We're going to stand right here to wash. Betsy says she'll take her clothes off, if you don't look."

Warmth rushed up his ears. "I'll wait over there." He jerked his thumb toward a wide sandy spot. "Thought I'd build a fire and make some coffee." The idea hadn't entered his mind until this very moment, but now it seemed good. He saw no sign of pursuit, and the child would want to get warm after her wash.

Crane lit the fire. He filled the coffeepot, opened a can of baked beans, and hunkered down on his heels.

Maggie carried the towel-wrapped child close to the fire and set her down on a grassy spot before she hung the wet underthings to dry and fetched a comb from her saddlebag. She perched behind the child on a fallen tree and combed the tangles from Betsy's wet hair.

Big brown eyes watched Crane as he stirred the beans, but as soon as he turned toward the child, she dipped her head and pulled the towel closer.

Maggie rested her hands on her thighs and looked across the fire to Crane. "She's nervous of you."

Crane thought on the notion, but before he could draw a conclusion, Maggie added, "She don't trust men." Her voice hardened. "She ain't got much reason to." She picked up the comb and ran her fingernail along the teeth, making an annoying insect sound.

Crane watched a play of emotions across her face. A look of

determination settled. "Don't worry, Child. This man won't hurt you. I promise." And the look she gave Crane was direct. He understood her meaning. *I'm making it my business to see you don't.*

He wanted to say not all men are the same, not all men want to treat her like that, but the child's frightened gaze stopped him. Instead he seated himself on a tree stump across the fire from Maggie and Betsy.

"Betsy," he began, the name awkward on his lips. "My name is Crane." She looked at a spot in the middle of his chest. "Maggie and I got married this morning." Now was not the time to wonder if he'd done the right thing. "We're headed west to the Territories, where we can get free land. We're going to build us a home and a new life. There'll be lots of work and not a lot of people. You're welcome to come with us if you want."

Maggie had finished combing Betsy's hair, and the girl turned to look into her face. "It's all right," Maggie said, rubbing her hands along the small arms. "We'll take good care of you." Crane nodded.

"Now turn around, and I'll braid your hair." The child obeyed instantly, plucking at the edge of the towel as Maggie worked on her hair and talked in a soothing tone. "I hear tell the grass is up to a horse's belly, and the mountains are giants topped with snow. They say the winters are cold, but the summers are so nice it's worth the winter just to get the summer."

Wondering where she'd picked up her information, Crane added, "There are ranches with thousands of cows. And deer and antelope." He'd seen many deer but was itching to see his first antelope.

"And flowers?" The child's eager question was so low Crane wondered if she'd really spoken. For a heartbeat he caught a glimpse of her big eyes before she ducked her head.

"Yup. Flowers, for sure." Though he'd never heard tell of them. But a country as pretty as the West was sure to have its share of flowers.

"And birds." He heard her sigh and met Maggie's solemn glance over her head.

Finished with Betsy's hair, Maggie stood and checked the garments. "Not dry yet," she announced. "That coffee ready?"

He filled two tin mugs with steaming coffee, then hesitated. "What about—?" He glanced toward Betsy. Maggie took her cup. "She can have water. Is there another cup?"

He shook his head. He never thought he'd have call for more than two.

"Doesn't matter."

He gulped some of the hot brew, then spooned beans onto the two plates, leaving his share in the can. He handed Maggie and Betsy each a plate and a biscuit. Maggie caught the child's fingers before they dug into the beans and wrapped them around the handle of a spoon.

As he ate, Crane kept a guarded eye on the pair across from him. Betsy licked up every crumb on her plate before turning to watch each mouthful he took. He swallowed hard. Betsy licked her fingertips. He tossed the almost-empty can at her.

"Here—wash this, and it can be your cup."

She dove after the can and cleaned it thoroughly with her fingers before she ran to the river and washed it.

"She's hungry," Maggie observed. "Wonder when she ate last."

"I'll open a can of peaches." He ambled to the packhorse and found what he wanted. When he returned, Betsy's eyes widened at what he held. He opened the can with his knife and poured almost half in her now-clean tin can and divided the rest between Maggie and him, keeping barely a taste for himself.

While he relaxed with his coffee, Maggie plucked the wisps of clothing from the nearby branches and took the child behind a curtain of trees to help her dress. When they emerged, Crane smiled. Betsy had all but disappeared in his shirt. The sleeves, rolled into a lump, hid her hands. Her bare toes flashed from under the garment. The neck hung over one shoulder. He glanced at Maggie, and seeing the amusement in her eyes, his smile widened.

Maggie washed the dishes and packed them away as Crane doused the fire. A few minutes later, they were back on the trail.

"I guess no one's after us," Maggie said, studying the back trail.

" 'Pears that way." But he knew he wouldn't relax for several days.

They headed west, Crane slouched in his saddle in the loose way that made the miles easy on the body. Used to long days in the saddle, he prepared to settle down into his own thoughts.

They had gone a mile or so when Betsy asked Maggie, "You got a mamma and papa?"

Crane strained to hear the conversation without indicating he listened, sensing neither Maggie nor Betsy would converse freely if they thought he could hear them.

Maggie didn't answer for a few minutes. "I had a mamma and papa."

"They was nice?" Her little voice quavered.

Crane eased back on the reins, dropping back half a gait.

Maggie lifted a hand and tugged at a strand of hair at her neck. "My mamma was real nice."

"What happened to her?"

Maggie shivered like a cold wind had torn across her neck and whispered, "She died two years ago."

"My mamma died too." Betsy twisted round and round the cuff of Crane's shirt she wore.

They rode on, the silence broken only by the thudding hooves of three horses and the cawing of a pair of crows disturbed by their presence.

"What happened to your papa?" Betsy asked.

Maggie's shoulders lifted and fell as she sighed. "He weren't the same after Mamma died."

"He beat you?" As much statement as question, the words made Crane clench his teeth.

"Sometimes." Maggie hesitated. "But I didn't mind that so much."

Betsy leaned around so she could look into Maggie's face. "What else he do?"

Maggie shook her head and refused to answer.

Crane's jaw started to ache.

"Guess he just didn't want us anymore," Maggie said after they had ridden several minutes.

"He was a bad man," Betsy said. "Like Bull."

"Bull?"

Betsy nodded.

"That the man who—?" Maggie began.

Betsy nodded, and again they rode in silence.

Finally Maggie spoke. "Well, Bull ain't never going to hurt you again. Ain't that right, Crane?"

Crane jerked to attention, meeting Maggie's challenging look. Betsy's glance slid away as soon as she saw him looking at her. "Yup. That's right."

Maggie stared at him a second longer, then nodded.

Satisfied he had given them the assurance they sought, Crane settled back. But something rattled at the back of his mind, something he'd missed, but he couldn't find it.

Betsy's thin voice broke the silence. "I never had a papa." She pulled Maggie's face close to whisper, barely loud enough for Crane to hear. "He have a mamma and papa?"

Maggie cast him a quick glance. "I don't know. You'll have to ask him yourself."

But the child hunched down. The horses walked on. When Crane determined neither female was going to ask the question of him, he gave his answer. "My parents are gone."

"Dead?" the child whispered.

He kept his eyes on the trail. "My mother died this winter past." He couldn't remember when she'd quit living.

"Your papa too?"

It seemed the child had a hankering to know about parents. He supposed he couldn't blame her, but it was something he no longer thought about. Finally he answered, "I don't know."

She nodded. "We's all orphans."

No one said anything different, and they rode on into the afternoon, passing scattered farmyards, houses, and barns set back from the road. Used to the quiet of the trail, Crane thought nothing of the silence until, turning to look toward one of the farms, he saw the child drooped over, her head wagging against Maggie.

She's sleeping. She's hardly bigger than a minute.

Maggie's head lulled from side to side. They were both asleep.

His first instinct was to rein in right now. But it wasn't a place to make camp.

Ahead he saw a farmhouse close to the trail and, hoping to get some supplies, turned toward the house.

When Maggie would have kept going straight ahead, he called her. She jerked up, saw his intent, and reined in to follow. Betsy lifted her head. Her face wrinkled as if she were going to cry, then she took a deep breath and pressed her quivering lips tight.

The woman of the house came to greet them, and a few minutes later they purchased eggs, potatoes, fresh bread, and a pie. As Crane secured the items in the packs, Betsy's round eyes followed him. Finally she could contain herself no longer.

"That all for us?"

He grinned. "You think we can handle it?"

Her stare greedily consumed the pie. "I only ever had pie once before."

"Didn't like it, huh?"

"Oh, yes. I did. It was so good." Her look said volumes more than her words did.

Until now Maggie had been silent. Now she grinned at Crane as she said to Betsy, "Don't suppose bread interests you?"

Betsy sighed in ecstasy. "I love bread."

"And eggs and potatoes?" Maggie prodded.

"And eggs and potatoes." The child swallowed hungrily.

"And just about anything you can put in your mouth," Maggie added, shaking her head.

Betsy gave Crane a desperate look. "I'm awful hungry."

Maggie's bubbling laughter caught Crane by surprise, sending tickling fingers up and down his spine. He ducked his head, mumbling, "We'll stop as soon as we find the right spot." He flicked the reins.

Behind him he heard Betsy. "We'll eat then, right?"

Crane grunted. It didn't take long before he saw what he wanted. "Over here." He pointed toward a bunch of trees.

He found a grassy spot close to the river and dropped from his horse. It was easy to see Maggie was about all done in, and he reached up to take Betsy, his hands completely encircling her tiny waist. As he lifted her, he made the alarming discovery she weighed even less than he'd estimated and swung her in a high, wide arc. His heart did a quick dogtrot. He felt her sharply indrawn breath.

I've scared the wee mite half to death! And just when we was starting to be friendly.

Her ribs quivered beneath his fingertips, and her voice quaked in a soft sound.

Now you done it. You made her cry.

He set her down, holding her until she gained her feet, but she hung limp in his arms, the same sound and the same quivering under his fingertips. He didn't know what to do and shot Maggie a look.

She stared at the child.

"I didn't think she'd be so light." He hoped Maggie would understand and forgive his stupidity.

She dragged her gaze to his.

But Betsy straightened, commanding his attention. She twisted in his grasp to look up at him, her tiny fingers clutching at his hands. "That was fun. Do it more." Her eyes shone, and she beamed up at him.

The thin sound and the shaking had been laughter. She wasn't scared; she had enjoyed it and begged for more.

"Again. Again." She bounced in his hands.

He didn't know what else to do, so he swung her up again, feeling the thistledown weight of her and hearing her thin laughter. When he finally released her, she spun around to face him. "I like that."

Crane rubbed his hands on the sides of his pants. He wondered if he should say something, but nothing came to mind. "Huh," he grunted finally, reaching up to help Maggie as she eased herself from the saddle. She didn't weigh a whole lot more than the child, but he felt something reassuring about her hands on his arms as she let him lower her to the ground. She tightened her grasp and bit her lip as she straightened.

"Didn't realize how hard I pushed us today," he murmured, knowing her discomfort was his fault.

"I'll be fine." And to prove her point, she dropped her hold on him.

They faced each other, a hum of thoughts knotting in the back of Crane's mind. "Guess I don't know nothing about traveling with a woman and child."

"You ever done it before?"

He pushed his hat back, trying to remember. "Can't say I recollect another time."

"Then, don't guess you'd know."

He nodded. It was all new to him. And not at all what he'd had in mind.

"Mind you," she continued, "I've never ridden west before." She paused. "And I've never had a husband before. So I guess we'll all have to learn as we go along."

"Right." He liked the sound of it. Kind of like easing into the whole thing.

three

He left them building a fire while he went to find meat, relishing the quiet of the open country. It gave him time to think. He was treading unfamiliar water. There was no guessing where the current would carry him next.

A brace of partridges shattered the air. He managed to bag two of them and carried them back to camp to prepare them.

Betsy ran to the water's edge to watch. "That for supper?"

"Yup."

"How long it gonna take to cook it?"

He glanced up and saw the pinched look around her mouth. "You hungry?"

She nodded, her eyes big.

"Think you can wait 'til it's cooked?"

"Maybe." She paused. "If it ain't too long."

He finished washing the carcasses, carried the birds to the fire, fixed them on a spit, and crouched down to tend them. Maggie dug a hole near the fire and put in three good-sized spuds, covering them with sand, then a layer of hot coals.

Betsy watched their every move, her hand twisting the bunched-up material at her wrists. "We have to wait now?"

Maggie answered. "It won't be long, Sweetie."

Still the child jittered inside Crane's too-large shirt. "We wouldn't have to wait for the pie to cook."

Crane stared at her, then looked at Maggie for direction, but Maggie only shrugged as if to say it was up to Crane.

"Why not?" he said.

The child's hands relaxed. Her smile was blinding.

Poor thing, he thought. *She must be starving.*

In an instant, he was a child again, older than her by a few years but still looking to his parents to provide food when necessary. He had climbed down the rough ladder to the basement and searched the bins for any overlooked vegetables, but he found nothing except a rotted carrot. The cupboards upstairs were as bare. His stomach hurt, though he couldn't be certain if it was from fear or hunger, and he huddled at the bottom of the ladder, hating to climb up and tell his mother nothing was left. No food and no money to buy it with.

He shook his thoughts aside. That was too long ago to think about. With the child's eager brown gaze on him, he retrieved the pie and cut it into six pieces. Betsy hung close, watching his every move.

"It's red," she said, leaning over as juice oozed out of the cut lines.

"Pieplant," he explained. "First fruit of the spring." His own taste buds were springing to life at the tangy smell of the pie.

"I like pieplant."

"You ever tasted it before?" he asked, lifting a piece to a tin plate.

"No, but I like it." Her eyes never left the wedge of pie.

Crane waited as she bit into it. At first taste, her mouth puckered, and her eyes grew round. Then the sweetness came, and she chewed greedily. He smiled. "You still like it?"

She raised her brown eyes to him and nodded, her mouth too full to speak.

Grinning, he served a wedge for Maggie and another for himself. "And a piece each for later," he said, setting aside the rest of the pie.

Crane thought Betsy would devour the delicacy in a gulp. Instead she lingered over every bite. He could almost feel her delight in the flavor and texture. When done, she licked her lips and handed the tin plate to Maggie. "That was good," she announced, then scampered to the river to cast stones in the water.

Maggie's clear laugh rang out. "My mother used to say, 'A child with a full tummy is a happy child.' "

Crane nodded. Hunger had a way of making everything else unimportant.

Maggie's smile faded. "I'm sure she meant children in a normal, happy family."

Again Crane nodded.

"Doesn't matter how full you are if you're scared to death." Her blue gaze drilled into him. "She'll never be afraid again," Maggie vowed.

"Not as far as it depends on us," Crane likewise vowed, meeting her piercing look with matching firmness.

Betsy played as Maggie and Crane turned their attention back to supper preparations. The partridges were soon spitting on the fire, the aroma bringing a flood of saliva to Crane's mouth and Betsy back to the fire.

"They almost ready?" she asked.

He looked up from turning the spit and, seeing the longing look on her face, laughed. "I thought you had enough pie in you to last awhile."

"It was good." She squirmed inside the too-big shirt. "But it's gone."

He knew she meant the feel of it in her stomach and nodded. "Guess you don't like nothing better than eating."

Her gaze lingering on the golden carcasses, she absently replied, "That's 'cause I'm hungry."

Struck by the simple wisdom of her words, he smiled. "You ever not hungry?"

With a look of fear making her brown eyes even browner, she faced him and solemnly shook her head.

He wanted to assure her everything would be all right now; yet sensing her fear of him, he settled for asking, "You ever had spit-roasted meat?"

She shook her head.

"Or roasted potatoes?"

Her eyes grew rounder, and she shook her head again.

He figured he could list a hundred things, and she'd continue to shake her head. "Well, get your plate. It's ready."

She dove for the plate.

"Slow down, Honey," Maggie crooned. "It's not going to disappear."

Crane cut a hunk of meat for Betsy. Maggie dropped a hot potato beside it. They ate in silence, both Maggie and Betsy eating as if there were no tomorrow. They finished and waited expectantly for him to pass the rest of the pie. Food took on an importance that hadn't existed for him since he got his first job. He wasn't paid much for sweeping the floor, carrying in wood and coal, and taking out ashes at the general store back home, but Mr. Brown had been only too happy to give him part of his wages in groceries. And after he moved on to bigger things, he always made certain his mother had a full pantry. Now all of a sudden he was faced with a child who was constantly hungry and a woman who ate like a workingman.

He ate his pie and straightened. Thank goodness they were passing through a country with plenty of game. He promised himself he would never let them go hungry.

Maggie and Betsy took the dishes to the river to wash, and Crane piled more wood close to the fire.

Dusk tiptoed in. It was time to get ready for the night. He untied the bedrolls from the pack, looking uncertainly at the bundles. He'd brought enough for two—man and wife—but what about the child? He could feel Betsy's stare boring into his back. The tension-filled air crackled.

"Betsy and I will sleep together, right, Betsy?" Maggie murmured. He could sense the child's relief as he handed Maggie a roll of blankets.

"Here you go, Honey." And giving her the bedroll, Maggie said, "You decide where we'll sleep." Crane chose a place close enough to the fire so he could throw on more wood if he got cold and against a fallen tree so he wasn't completely exposed. With a flick of his wrists, he spread the roll on the ground.

When he returned from checking the horses, Betsy still stood clutching the blankets. Her glance darted away when he looked at her. He poured himself another cup of coffee and took it to his pallet. He removed his boots, setting them carefully against the tree trunk, put his hat on top, and stood the rifle close before he settled down on the pad to enjoy the coffee.

"You pick a spot?" Maggie urged the child.

She nodded.

"Well, then?"

Still Betsy stood rooted there, her big eyes watching Crane. He made a point of ignoring her, letting her feel her space and decide what she wanted. He heard a little sigh before she silently eased in his direction. She halted so close he could tell she was breathing through her mouth. Then she knelt down and set the blankets next to his, struggling to unroll them.

Maggie knelt beside her to help. "You sure this is where you want to sleep?"

It was the same question Crane wanted to ask.

Betsy nodded without looking up.

"There's lots of other places," Maggie insisted.

"I know," the child whispered. "This is the best."

Maggie stared at her.

Crane watched them both from beneath his eyelashes.

"This is a fine spot all right," Maggie agreed, "But can you tell me why you picked it?"

Betsy glanced sideways at Maggie and whispered, "So we can be close to him." She flung a quick glance at Crane. "He takes care of us."

The child's words slammed into him. He steadied his cup, keeping his eyes lowered.

Maggie jerked to her feet. "You need anything before you go to bed?" she asked the child.

"Can I have a drink?"

Maggie handed her a cup. "Run get some water from the river. Mind you, don't get your clothes wet."

The child scampered away.

Crane lifted his head to face Maggie. Her fists thudded against her hips, and she glowered at him.

"What?" he asked, having no notion what had made her angry.

"It seems you've earned the trust of the child."

She made it sound as if he'd done something wrong. "So?"

"So?" she repeated. "The trust of a child is a precious thing."

He nodded.

"Some people act like it's nothing. They don't take it into consideration." She was breathing hard.

Again he nodded, having no idea what she was trying to say but figuring it wasn't a good time to point it out.

"You have a child. You got to always be there."

It was a sucker punch, but he knew what she meant. "I ain't going no place."

Betsy sang as she returned.

Maggie's eyes narrowed as she drove her words home. "You earned the trust of that child. See you live up to it." And as Betsy stepped into the light, she turned to her. "You ready for bed now?"

He crawled under the covers, turning his back to give the other two privacy, aware when Betsy crawled in next to him, the cold from her bare feet reaching out to the small of his back. Maggie settled in next to the child.

"Go to sleep," she murmured, hands brushing along Crane's spine as she pulled the covers around the child.

Crane let his body settle into the shape of the ground and waited for sleep to envelop him, but tonight sleep did not come instantly. Instead his thoughts hovered on the day. He'd been so confident of what he was doing when he rode into town. Now he couldn't say exactly what he'd expected; only it wasn't anything like this.

He guessed he thought he would marry, and somehow, come nighttime, they would crawl under the covers together, and the rest would come natural. But instead they lay under separate covers, a child between them. Perhaps it was as it should be. After all, what did he know about being married? He couldn't even look at his parents for an example. His father had left when he was eleven. He could only remember what it was like afterward. And his adult life had taken him on the trail with other drifters and cows. He hadn't had a lot of women in his life.

The feeling he had was not unlike grabbing on to the tail of a stampede.

He was awakened by an unfamiliar sound and something touching him. He jerked up, reaching for his rifle before he realized it was a pair of bare feet kicking at him. And the sound was the child sobbing. He waited for Maggie to do something, but by the gentle snores from her direction, he knew she hadn't been disturbed by the noise.

How much did it take to wake her? he wondered.

The sobs bordered on hysteria. Betsy must be having a nightmare.

"Betsy." He touched her shoulder. She jerked away, choking on a scream.

"Betsy." He shook her. "Wake up."

Still sobbing, she reached for him, pulling herself to his lap, huddling against his chest.

He stiffened, afraid to touch her. She was so small. But her sobs shuddered through him, and not knowing what else to do, he wrapped his arms around her, cradling her. "Shh. You're safe now. Stop crying. Stop crying."

Maggie grunted and sat up, rubbing her eyes. "What's going on?"

"The child was having a bad dream."

Maggie reached out to rub Betsy's back. "It's only a dream, Honey."

Together they comforted the child, and her sobs quieted. Crane held her as her breathing deepened.

"She's asleep again," he whispered.

Maggie pulled the covers back so he could lower Betsy to her bed. Their hands brushed as they smoothed the blanket over the sleeping girl.

"She'll be fine now," Maggie whispered.

Crane went to the fire and shoved wood into the embers. Sparks flared, and he saw Maggie standing close, her arms wrapped around her middle, her eyes watchful. He shook the coffeepot. It rattled with dry grounds.

"I'll make more," Maggie offered.

"No need." He settled on a stump, staring at the flames.

Maggie pulled a piece of log close and sat beside him. "Are you having regrets?" she asked, her voice low.

"About what?"

"About everything. Getting married." She hesitated. "To me." Another pause. "About the child."

He laughed. "More like confused. Not in my wildest dreams was this what I expected. I'm wondering what's going to happen next."

"Bet you thought your first night as a married man would be a little different, huh?"

He could feel warmth creep up his neck and thanked the darkness she couldn't see it. "I really hadn't given it a lot of thought."

The soft night noises settled around them.

Finally Maggie said, "I guess it's my fault."

He shrugged. "You didn't force me to do anything." Then he added, "Tonight is only the first night of the rest of our lives. We got lots of time."

He felt her sigh and looked across the fire to the sleeping child, barely a ripple under the blankets. "You think she'll be all right?" he asked.

"I don't know. What do you think?"

"I know nothing about little ones, but she seems eager to find good things and enjoy them. I think she'll do fine."

"I think you're right. Besides, she's young. The younger you are, the easier it is to forget."

He thought about that. For certain he didn't remember much about his younger years. In fact, he'd thought about his youth more today than he had in a long time. Maybe, he admitted, he'd done his best to forget those early years. Meeting this child had driven his thoughts to those forgotten places.

"We best get some sleep." He waited for her to cross to the child's side, then followed.

Throughout the night he was aware of the child beside him, her little snufflings and sighings and her feet pressing into his side. He couldn't decide whether or not he liked it, but he was certain it kept him half awake all night.

&

He tensed at the humming sound close to his ear and dragged his eyes open. Betsy sat cross-legged almost at his head.

"I'm hungry," she announced when she saw his eyes open.

He groaned. "You're always hungry."

She waited and, when he made no move, asked, "Aren't you hungry?"

"Where's Maggie?"

"She's sleeping. I tried to make her wake up."

He grunted. That left him to deal with this persistent scrap of humanity. "You got coffee ready?"

She giggled. "I can't make coffee."

"Time you learned." He rolled to his feet and stretched. "First thing you do every morning is make coffee."

She nodded and scampered to the ashes of last night's fire. Grabbing the coffeepot, she turned with a questioning look.

"Take it to the river and wash it out and fill it with fresh water."

She was gone in a flash, and he set about getting the fire going. The wood was dry and caught instantly.

As he waited for the child to return, he looked at Maggie's sleeping form, again wondering what it took to waken her. She lay on her side, her hands curled together under her chin, her black hair fanned out around her face. In repose she looked even younger. He felt a swell of doubt; then he reminded himself she'd proven to be more than resourceful and strong. The way she had gone after that man back at Colhome—he grinned. She was like a bantam rooster.

Betsy nudged his leg. "I got your water."

"Thanks." He took the pot and dumped in a handful of grounds and set it over the fire. "Now we wait."

He hunkered down. Betsy did the same.

For a moment she was content to watch. Then she looked at him. "Isn't it time to start some food?"

He chuckled. "What would you like? Eggs, or"—he paused, smiling at the eager look on her face—"or eggs?"

"I like eggs."

"I bet you do." He'd gamble she'd never met a food she didn't like. He glanced at Maggie, still breathing deeply. "Looks like you're my number one helper."

Betsy quivered with anticipation. "I can help."

"Right." He went to the packs and pulled out a spider. "You take this to the fire."

"It looks funny. What is it?" she asked, holding up the cast-iron skillet.

"Spider. See the legs on the bottom. Works real well over a fire." He grabbed the rest of the biscuits and carried the eggs himself. With Betsy sticking close as an August fly, he set the spider over the fire and checked on the coffee.

"You better get Maggie awake before I start the eggs."

Her response was instantaneous. "Maggie, Maggie!" she yelled, racing over to pummel Maggie's arm. "Get up so we can have breakfast."

Maggie moaned. "I'm awake, Betsy. You can stop pounding me."

"Your eyes aren't open." Betsy shook her.

One eye squinted open. "There. That suit you?"

"You got to get up. Crane says we can't eat 'til you do."

"He does, does he?" She squinted at him. "You sure it's morning already?"

"Yes, it is. See—the sun is coming up." Betsy pointed to the east.

Maggie closed her eyes and pulled the covers to her chin. "That settles it. It isn't morning 'til the sun is up all the way."

"Maggie, please." Betsy pulled at the covers. "I'm hungry."

"And I'm so tired." Her voice was muffled.

Betsy gave Crane a look of desperation, and he said, "Maybe I should get a bucket of water from the river and dump it on her."

Betsy sprang to her feet, silently urging him to do it, and Maggie jerked upright.

"You wouldn't." She glowered at him.

He chuckled. "Looks like I don't need to."

With a scowl darkening her features, she sat in the midst of her rumpled blankets.

"Guess I can start the eggs now," he said to Betsy, who hurried to his side, watching his every move as he cracked shells and dropped eggs into the sizzling pan.

Behind them Maggie groaned and stood to her feet, shuffling to the river to splash cold water on her face.

When she returned, Crane offered her a cup. "Coffee's hot and strong."

For several minutes she nursed it without speaking. He observed her out of the corner of his eye, amazed as she slowly came to life. Like a flower opening to the sun!

"Get the dishes," he told Betsy, and she ran to obey.

"She sleep the rest of the night?" Maggie spoke low.

"Yup. And woke up before the birds, complaining she was hungry."

Maggie chuckled. "Did you see how she ate last night?"

Crane raised his eyebrows.

She nodded. "I know. I ate a lot too." She ducked her head. "I was hungry."

He grinned. "You hungry now?" Taking the plates Betsy had fetched, he dished up their breakfast.

She grimaced. "It's too early to eat."

Betsy cleaned her plate, ate three biscuits, and when she saw Maggie hadn't eaten all her eggs, asked, "You finished, Maggie?"

Maggie handed her plate to Betsy.

The sun was completely over the horizon, and already

Crane could feel its heat. "Let's get moving."

Betsy and Maggie cleaned the dishes, rolled up the bedrolls, and filled the canteens, while Crane caught and saddled the horses and fixed the packs. Then they were ready. But when Maggie reached for Betsy, the child ducked away to stand at Crane's side.

"I want to ride with you."

With studied calmness, Crane continued checking the cinches and determined no one would see how her request had surprised him. How could she have changed so suddenly from the child who wouldn't even look at him yesterday? He didn't understand it, but it made him feel warm inside. He kind of liked the feeling. But he didn't know if he could trust it.

"Come on then." He scooped her up, bringing a squeal as he tossed her to Rebel's back before climbing up behind her. He flashed Maggie a look, watching to see if she'd been hurt by Betsy's choice.

Maggie smiled. "It's fine by me."

"Let's make tracks," he called, heading down the trail with the sun warming their backs.

Betsy squirmed from side to side, trying to take in everything around her. "Crane, Crane, look—a rabbit!" she called as a brown jackrabbit sprang from the grass. And a few minutes later, "Crane, Crane, look. A whole bunch of yellow flowers."

"Yup," Crane answered. "You better sit still before you fall."

"You'd catch me, wouldn't you, Crane?"

"Depends." *How do you catch thistledown?*

For a few minutes she sat still, then looked at him over her shoulder. "Crane, does everybody have a papa?"

"Yup. Everybody's got to."

"Why do papas go?"

The question flashed down the pathway of his mind to a bewildered boy who asked himself a similar question. *Why did my papa leave?* There had never been an answer, and he had soon found life went on, leaving no time to dwell on it.

"Not all papas leave."

She shook her head. "Mammas die. Papas leave."

How could he convince her otherwise? He flung a desperate look at Maggie.

"She's only going by what she knows. We've all lost our mothers." She paused. "I told her my pa didn't want me around."

Crane watched her through narrowed eyes. Did he see a flash of pain just then? Or had she, like he, learned to accept the reality of a father who didn't care? Was two years long enough to grapple with the problem and learn to leave it be? Maggie looked directly at him. "I don't recall for sure what you said about your father."

He stared into her blue eyes, again struck by how little they knew of each other. "He left when I was eleven. It was a long time ago." The future beckoned. Let the past be past.

Maggie nodded, her eyes intent for another heartbeat. Then she said, "Guess you can hardly blame her for how she thinks." She dropped her gaze to Betsy, who strained to catch their every word. "Honey, Crane's right. Not all papas leave."

"They stay forever?" Her whispered awe tugged at an unfamiliar emotion in Crane.

"That's right," he agreed.

"Forever," she whispered. "That sounds nice."

They rode for several minutes before she asked, "There a house where we're going?"

"Not yet. We'll build one when we get there."

"A real house with rooms?"

"Yup."

"A kitchen?" she persisted.

"Yup."

"A parlor?" She rolled the word around in her mouth. "And a room for me?"

"A house just right for us."

"Us." Her chest heaved, and she settled again.

They continued in comfortable silence until Betsy asked, "How long to get there?"

Up until now, Crane hadn't given it a great deal of thought.

He'd estimated it to be about eight hundred miles from Manitoba to the plains facing the mountains in the Territories. But now, as he explained the distance to Betsy and saw her look of disbelief, he realized how far it sounded to a child. "I hope we'll find a place by the end of June."

"Not tomorrow?"

"No."

"Not the day after?" Her shoulders slumped.

Maggie came to his rescue. "We'll see lots and lots of things. It's like a picnic every day."

Betsy nodded. Crane sensed her disappointment and longed to say something to dispel it, but he could think of nothing to make the trip seem shorter. Her head nodded. At first he thought she was still quietly thinking about the trip. Then, as she slumped to one side, he realized she had fallen asleep and, pulling her toward him, let her rest on his chest. Maggie smiled at the sleeping child, then at him, and Crane felt something unfamiliar, yet not altogether unwelcome, burgeon in a spot slightly below his throat.

He let Betsy sleep until it was time to stop. They had cold leftover partridge and the last of the bread. Not wanting to take time to build a fire, they settled for a drink of cool water.

As soon as she had eaten, Betsy ran along the riverbank, yelling tunelessly with her arms outflung. She ran until a pile of rocks stopped her progress. Then she turned and ran back, still yelling and waving her arms.

Maggie watched, grinning. "She's glad to be feeling her legs under her."

Crane turned from checking the cinches and stared after the child. He hadn't given the long hours in the saddle a thought, finding riding more comfortable than walking. Again he realized how little he knew about traveling with a child and a woman. He turned to Maggie. "You getting pretty sore of riding too?" He'd noticed her awkward way of walking.

It was a moment before she faced him. "I'm not used to

it." Her blue gaze held steady, making it clear she wasn't complaining.

He ducked behind Rebel. "I 'spect we could walk some."

Crane led the way. With a narrow path along the river, they had no need to return to the trail.

Betsy ran ahead, then stopped suddenly, turning toward him, her face bright. "Listen to the birds," she whispered. "They sound so happy."

Crane halted. He'd never bothered to listen much unless the birds raised a fuss, then he would check to see why. But now he really listened.

The child stood with her face lifted, her eyes closed. It made his chest tighten just to watch her.

"It must be great to be so young and be able to forget your past as easily as she does." Maggie tugged Liberty's reins. "Let's get moving."

"Yup," he drawled. "I'm looking forward to crossing into the Territories." But it was nice walking, he decided. Betsy ran and skipped like a heifer released from the barn. Even the silence between him and Maggie was pleasant. And it was cooler next to the river. They walked until Betsy's steps began to slow. Then they returned to the trail. Crane knew enough now to begin planning the evening camp early in the afternoon. So when he saw a farm close to the road, he turned in.

A thin, worried-looking woman came from the house.

"I'm looking to buy some food," Crane called. "You got anything to spare?"

Before she could answer, an overalled man came from around a low building. "We got some pork and eggs." He named a price that made Crane raise his eyebrows.

"You be fixing to skin us?" Crane asked.

"I've no mind to leave my own family short," the man growled. "But you're mor'n welcome, if you've a mind to pay."

Crane stared hard at the man. If he'd been alone, he would have turned his back and ridden away, but with two hungry females to feed and them already wilting, he jerked his head in agreement.

"Run and get it, Missus," the farmer ordered his wife, and she scurried inside, returning with a hunk of meat and a sack of eggs. Crane unwrapped the paper from the meat and sniffed. Satisfied it was unspoiled, he handed a fistful of change to the man and turned to leave, passing between several low outbuildings.

"Phew. It stinks." Betsy wrinkled her nose as they neared a pigpen, knee-deep in muck.

"Hush," he ordered, determined not to offend the man he sensed thrived on trouble.

"Look at that boy," Betsy said. "He's stuck in it."

"No, he's not," he said, though it took a great deal of effort for the lad to carry two heavy buckets of feed through the slop without upsetting them.

With a muffled gasp, Maggie slid from her horse and rushed to the fence. "Ted!" she called as she struggled to unlatch the gate.

The boy looked at her with blank eyes.

"Ted, Ted." She pulled on the heavy gate. "It's me. Maggie."

four

The boy changed his grip on the handle of the bucket and continued toward the trough, pigs squealing at his heels.

"Ted, wait!" Maggie called, jerking at the gate and squeezing through the wedge opening.

"Maggie." Even as he uttered the low warning, Crane figured she'd ignore it. "Here we go again," he muttered, pushing his hat back.

"What's she doing?" Betsy asked, her voice thin and shrill as Maggie lifted her skirts and plunged into the muck. "Oh, yuck, yuck!" Betsy pulled her face down into the neckline of the shirt she wore.

The smell stinging his eyes, Crane shifted so he could see Maggie and watch for the farmer.

Maggie reached the boy. "Ted, listen." Her voice was taut. "It's me, Maggie. I thought I'd never find you."

When the boy acted as if she hadn't spoken, she wrenched the bucket from his hands and flung it away. The pigs oinked after it, their noise drowning out her words as she grasped his shoulder.

The boy raised his head, but his eyes stared away as if sightless.

Crane, wondering if the boy was deaf, watched the farmer approach, a shotgun tucked under his arm. Crane eased his hand toward his rifle.

The man stood before the twisted gate. "Leave the boy be," he growled. "He's got work."

"He's my brother." She grabbed the boy's hand and tugged at him to follow. "I've looked for him for so long."

"Your father sold him to me fair and square. Said he was mine to do with as I wanted."

46

Crane's jaw tightened. From the boy's bony thinness, he guessed feeding him wasn't one of the things the man did. In fact, he'd guess the boy was treated worse than the animals. "How much?" Crane growled.

The man jerked toward him. "How much what?"

"For the boy." It stuck in his throat to say it.

A gleam brightened the other man's eyes. "I paid twenty dollars for him." He scratched his nose. "Figuring all I put into him, he should be worth twice that."

"He's my brother," Maggie cried, approaching the gate. "He belongs with me."

The farmer lifted his shotgun and pointed it at her. "Don't see him agreeing."

"Ted, tell them. Tell them you're Edward Malone, my brother."

The pigs squealed, the man snorted, but the boy made not a sound. Crane pulled out a twenty-dollar bill. "This should do it."

The man lowered the gun, snatched the money, and put it in his overalls. "He ain't much use anyway," he snarled. "The boy's addled."

"He ain't!" Maggie cried. "He's fine."

"He can ride with you." Crane led the mare to Maggie's side, holding the reins as she pulled herself into the saddle. She reached down for the boy, but he neither looked at her nor lifted his hand.

Crane reined closer and lifted the boy up behind Maggie. "Ride downwind," he ordered as they rode from the farmyard.

But even with two lengths between them, the smell was almost unbearable. Betsy clung to him, her nose buried in the neckline of her shirt. The distance between him and Maggie made conversation impossible. Crane was more than willing to wait.

He led them into the river, not turning until Liberty stood knee-deep in it. Then he reined back to shore. "Get rid of that smell." He set Betsy down and dropped to the ground beside her.

"What they going to do?" Her voice was thin.

"Wash, I hope." He removed the saddle, took the packs from the other horse, and led both animals to water. When they'd had their fill, he tethered them to graze.

Betsy's wide eyes followed his every move.

"You gather up some branches for the fire. Mind you, don't go too far." He dug a curry brush from the pack.

"Then we'll have supper?"

"Soon." He trod back to the river to catch Liberty and set to scrubbing the manure from the stirrups. "No need to carry this smell west with us," he muttered.

Satisfied the saddle was clean, he carried it to shore and hung it over a stump. Then he returned and scrubbed Liberty, sparing a glance at Maggie and her brother.

She faced him, hands on hips. "Ted, you got to take off those clothes. Let me help you." She reached out. His arms tightened at his sides. "I'll wash them, and you can have them back," she pleaded. He remained stiff. "Maybe Crane can give you something to wear while they dry." She shot a glance toward him.

He nodded and retraced his steps to the saddles, digging out a faded blue shirt and tossing it beside the towel on the bank. "It's my last one," he mumbled, turning his back, running his hands over the horse, watching without appearing to. "Your sister only wants to help, young man." He bent and rinsed the brush. "And a bath wouldn't do you no harm."

He put his attention on washing Liberty's flank but could see out of the side of his vision as Maggie grasped the boy's shirt and pulled it over his head. The boy did not resist; neither did he help.

"Ted, you imagine how scared I was when I came home and found you was gone." She urged him out of his trousers. "Pa was gone too. No one seemed to know where you was." She turned him around and gasped, flicking a glance at Crane.

Crane saw what she had, the angry red welts across the boy's back. As his pants lowered, he took in the gaunt ribs, the bruises across the buttocks. Crane's insides twisted into a knot.

Maggie shuddered, then gently lathered soap over the thin body. She talked as she worked. "It took me three days to find Pa in a back alley. He didn't much like it when I tried to make him tell me where you were." She paused to splash clean water over the boy. "Well, you know what he was like after Ma died, and he took to the bottle." She led him to the sandy bank. "He said he sold you, but he couldn't remember the man's name or where he lived."

She picked up the towel, draping it over his shoulders. But when she would have hugged him, he shrugged away and stared past Maggie without so much as a blink. Maggie drew in a sharp breath.

Crane led Liberty to the other horses. The river murmured past. Betsy added more branches and twigs to the pile she'd made. Her voice carried on the gentle breeze, and Crane paused to listen. She was singing a song she had made up.

"Pie, pie, I like pie. I like flowers and the birds that fly. I like everything. But I like pie the best of all." Her voice was clear and sweet.

Crane smiled as he tethered the horse. He cut off thick slabs of the hunk of pork and fried it in the hot spider. The rest he put into a large pot, covered it with water, and threw in a handful of salt and one bay leaf.

"Why'd you put in a leaf?" Betsy demanded.

He settled back on his heels, and Betsy squatted beside him. Across the fire Maggie nursed a cup of coffee, her expression troubled. The boy huddled on the ground in Crane's shirt, his body turned away from the rest of them as if to shut them out. "It's a trick Biscuit taught me." He stirred the pot and put on a lid.

"Biscuit?"

"Yup. The best camp cook I ever knew." He glanced around the circle again. No one seemed to have anything to offer, so he continued. "He was as mangy looking as an old dog. Not one you'd pick to cook your meals. But he made the best biscuits I ever had." He bent his glance to Betsy's. "That's how he come to be called Biscuit."

He paused to scratch his chin. "Never did know what his rightful name was."

Betsy bounced on her heels. "He the one who told you to put a leaf in?"

"Yup. It's a bay leaf. Adds a little flavor." He lifted the lid to see if the water had boiled yet.

"For sure?"

"Yup."

"Then I like leaves." She skipped around the fire to Maggie. "You too, Maggie?" She leaned close, touching Maggie's face.

Maggie smiled at her and nodded.

"You sad?" the child asked. "About him?" She nodded toward Ted, who gave no indication of hearing.

Again Maggie nodded.

Betsy straightened and walked to Ted's side. She put her face close to him. "You don't need to be afraid anymore. Maggie and Crane will take care of you."

The boy jerked away, turning his back to her. His foot thrashed out, catching Betsy in the ankle and knocking her to the ground.

Whimpering, Betsy jumped up and backed away.

Maggie stood to her feet. "Ted. What are you doing? You mustn't hurt Betsy." But when she lifted a hand to touch him, he shrank back. Seeing his fear, Maggie turned to let her hand fall on Betsy instead. "Are you okay, Honey?"

Betsy nodded. Crane reached out and turned the frying meat before he walked around the fire to face Ted. "I think it's time we introduced ourselves. I'm Byler Crane, but everyone calls me Crane. You can too." He paused, waiting. "Me and your sister are married."

The boy gave no sign he heard.

"We's headed west to start a new life."

Still nothing.

"We found Betsy in a town back there. She needed someone.

She's coming with us." He was beginning to wonder what he would have to do to get the boy's attention. "You're more than welcome to throw in with us." He waited. "Unless you've a mind to go back to that pig farmer."

The narrow shoulders hunched forward just enough for Crane to nod. At least he could be certain the boy understood what was said.

"I thought not. Then I guess you're stuck with us."

He turned back to the fire, pouring himself a cup of coffee. "On a long trail every hand has to do his share." He downed the scalding cup of coffee, poured his cup full again, and shook the pot. "Almost empty," he announced. "Guess we need some more water."

Betsy sprang to her feet, but Crane said, "Ted, how 'bout you fill it at the river? Mind you, go upstream from where the horses are." He held out the pot.

The boy stiffened.

Maggie half stood, but Crane shook his head, hoping she'd understand this was something he had to settle with Ted.

The boy jumped to his feet so quickly, Crane blinked. He snatched the pot and raced toward the river.

Crane could almost hear the boy's thoughts. *You can make me do it, but you can't make me like it.* He smiled. If beneath those glassy eyes was a fighter, so much the better.

He opened two cans of beans and set them to heat.

"Is it almost ready?" Betsy hovered at his side.

He studied her. She seemed none the worse for having been knocked down by Ted. "As soon as Ted's back."

She squatted beside him. "Ted's mad?"

He met Maggie's eyes. "I'm not sure," he answered. Maggie stared after her brother.

Betsy spoke again. "I think that man hurt him."

Crane stiffened, wondering if she had seen the marks on Ted's back.

The child continued, "He's a bad man. Like Bull."

"He'll never hurt him again," Maggie muttered.

Ted returned, holding the coffeepot toward Crane without looking at him.

"Thanks, Boy." Crane poured in the coffee, then dished up the food. He'd eat his own out of the spider.

He handed the plates around. Betsy dug into her food without hesitation, but Maggie waited, watching as he handed a plate to Ted. The boy jerked back as if expecting to be hit.

"Food," Crane said. "Enjoy."

Ted grabbed the plate, turning away his shoulders as if to shut them out again.

Maggie sat close to him. "You're safe now, Ted," she murmured. "We'll take good care of you, Crane and I."

Ted gobbled up his food without any indication he'd heard.

Betsy scampered down to the water to play, her laughter and singing whispering through the dusk. Ted disappeared into the trees, gathering more firewood. Crane filled Maggie's cup, then hunched down to enjoy his own coffee. She edged closer.

"I couldn't leave him."

He watched her in the dancing light. A shower of sparks hissed, their light flashing through her hair. "Any more surprises?"

Her eyes grew round; her cheeks darkened. Then she smiled. "Don't think so."

He'd noticed before how a smile made her look so good he could hardly breathe.

"Ted used to be—" Her voice was tight. "He used to be—"

He nodded. "How old is he? How long since you saw him?"

Maggie sniffed. "He's ten now. It's been eight, no ten months, since I've seen him." She shuddered. "Did you see his back?"

He nodded. "Met a few men who liked to hurt others. Just a few, but that was a few too many."

"He was eight when Ma died, and Pa—well, Pa changed. We never saw much of him, and when we did, he was mean. I was glad when he left us alone."

Maggie threw the rest of her coffee in the fire. Over the

hissing protest, she growled, "I don't care if I never see our pa again."

Crane drained his cup. There wasn't much he could say to that. Best to get on with life, he always figured. He was about to remind her about the new life in the West, freedom and all that, when she asked, "Why didn't anyone help him?"

"Most people don't want to start trouble."

"Seems to me it was already started."

He kept his gaze on the fire, but he could feel her stare knifing into him. He gnawed on his bottom lip, wondering how her mouth would feel to kiss. Here he was a married man for two days now, and he hadn't even kissed his bride. Come to think of it, this was the first time they'd been alone since the wedding. And about high time he had his first kiss. He set his cup down at his feet and twisted toward her.

Her blue eyes caught the flare of light from a leaping flame and shot silver spears. Her lips were parted, but as he turned, she spoke. "Would you ignore a child in trouble? Would you have ridden past Ted?"

He pulled in a cooling breath and swallowed hard, dismissing the idea of a kiss. Later, he promised himself. "I don't know." *Of course I would and never give him a backward look.*

"What if it was you?"

"Me?"

"Yes, what if you needed someone to help? What if you were that child?"

He twitched, feeling like a knife had been plunged into his solar plexus. The occasional word of Betsy's song reached him. Behind him in the brush he could hear the crack of branches as Ted stepped on them. Flames licked the air. Sparks exploded, sizzling through the night.

"I was that child." He hadn't meant to say it out loud, but it couldn't be lassoed back.

"What?"

"Things got tough after my pa left. Some days we didn't have enough to eat." *Never enough, and lots of times nothing at all.*

"And no one helped you?"

"I don't remember thinking they should." And once he started to work, they always had food. He never looked back.

"I will never walk by a child in trouble and not stop to ask if I can do anything." Crossing her arms, she glared at him.

"It's a mighty good thing you told me this." He narrowed his eyes. *Wonder what other little philosophies she has hidden up her sleeve.*

For a moment more she glared at him. Then she giggled. "Guess you already figured it out." She sobered. "I didn't mean to cause you so much trouble."

He shrugged, then refilled their cups. She moved over on the log, making room for him. They sat side by side, staring into the flames. Her shoulder whispered against his arm. She seemed so small beside him. He was certain he could wrap his arms around her with plenty of room to spare.

Her hair had a fresh summer-day scent, and he breathed deeply. He wanted to draw her close. But he sat as still as the log on which they perched, uncertain how she would react. A nerve twitched in his arm. Maybe she was wanting this as much as he.

"Do you believe in God?"

"What?" If she wasn't the blamedest one for talking all the time.

"I said, do you believe in God? I guess you must, seeing as you wanted a God-fearing woman for a wife."

He sighed. " 'Course I do. My mother taught me it was so."

Maggie nodded. "Mine too. What all did she tell you about Him?"

Crane tried to remember. "She said things like God made everything. She said He would take care of us. Other things." It was so long ago.

Maggie grabbed his arm, sending warm waves along its length. "What did she say about Him taking care of us?"

Pa had been gone a few days, maybe a week—he couldn't

remember for sure—but long enough that Crane had grown suspicious.

"Where's Pa?" he'd demanded yet again.

His mother turned away but not before Crane caught the flash of pain in her face. "He's away."

"Is he coming back?" Crane insisted. He had to get rid of the awful feeling in the pit of his stomach.

But she had turned slowly. "Come sit by me, Byler. I've something to tell you."

Inside he had screamed, "No! I don't want to hear it!" But he let his mother draw him to the big old armchair and pull him to her lap.

"I don't know when your pa is coming back."

The pain in his stomach erupted.

"But I know he will come back." She smiled as she brushed his hair from his forehead. "Because I prayed about it. And God has said He'd take care of us, so I know He'll send Tom back. I promise you." She stroked his forehead, her words driving back the pain.

But Pa had not come back.

That was the last time his mother had held him. It was the last time he believed a promise.

Maggie tugged at his arm. "Tell me what she said, what she meant."

Ignoring the stabbing in his belly, Crane said, "After Pa left, she prayed. She said she knew God would bring him back. She hoped and hoped, but when he didn't come back, she began to die inside."

At first, he had thought she was angry with him, that somehow it was his fault Pa had left. That was why she no longer laughed with him, or tickled him, or told him jokes. It was years before he figured out it was because of her own heartbreak. Not until now did he realize she simply couldn't survive without hope.

In happier times she had read the Bible and talked about God. In his mind he was certain the two were connected.

"I got something you might like to see." He pushed to his feet. Digging in the saddlebags, he found a paper-wrapped parcel and took it to her.

She turned it over in her hands. "What is it?"

"Open it and see."

Maggie's fingers danced at the knots, then she unfolded the crackling paper. "It's a Bible," she whispered, trailing her fingertips over the black leather.

"It was my mother's." A smile tugged at the corners of his mouth. "She wanted me to take it." He'd been home on one of his visits. In the months since he'd last seen her, she had failed noticeably.

"One of these days you won't be needing to come back here. You can follow those cows and that trail as far as you like," she'd said. "Son, I wish you all the best. I wish life could have been better for you, but"—she sighed—"keep my Bible with you always. Read it. Maybe you'll do better than me in learning God's ways."

After her death he had disposed of her meager belongings but, remembering his promise, had packed the Bible for the trip west.

Eyes wide and bright, Maggie stared at him a moment, then turned back to the Bible. "My ma always wanted a Bible. She said her folks back in the old country had one." Slowly she opened the pages. "I can't believe I'm actually holding one." She turned page after page, letting her hand slide over each. "It's so beautiful."

The pages fell open at the center, and she tipped the book toward the flames so she could see better. Crane watched as she read the black spidery names in the family tree. "Thomas Crane was your father."

"Yup."

"Powell Crane?" She looked at him again.

"My brother. He was born four years before me. He only lived six months."

She looked away. "How awful." A shudder shook her.

Then her finger trailed up the page. "Imagine being able to see all your family like this for all these years gone by." She fixed a searching look on him. "It must make you feel good."

Crane rocked back on his heels as he considered it. All his life he'd been a loner. He hadn't given family a lot of thought, except occasionally to acknowledge to himself that his mother's dependency tethered him to his home. But Maggie's words hit a mark. "I guess it's kind of nice."

Satisfied, she nodded. The sound of crashing wood echoed across the clearing, and Crane turned to see Ted wipe bark and leaves from his arms, a pile of branches at his feet. In the dimming light the boy looked even bonier, his face all sharp angles. Crane glanced toward the trees. Darkness had fallen as they talked.

"Time to call the children in," he murmured even as Maggie called, "Ted, stay here now. That's enough wood, thanks."

On the heels of her voice, Crane called out, "Betsy, come in now."

"Coming." The light voice carried through the dusk, then she could be heard singing, the words and voice growing more distinct as she skipped toward them.

"Look what I found." She knelt at Maggie's side and unwound her objects from the rolled-up shirttail. "A shiny rock and this one all full of holes." She set them at her knees. "And look." She held up a twisted piece of driftwood rubbed soft by the water. "It's so pretty." She lifted it toward Crane. "Isn't it, Crane?"

He smiled. "It sure is." Even so young, she was quick to let go of the past and rush wholeheartedly into the future.

Scooping up her treasures, Betsy sprang to her feet and scampered to the far side of the fire where Ted sat as still as a stone. "Look, Ted. See all the nice things I found." She held them out for him to examine. "There's lots of good things down there. You should come with me next time."

Ted lifted his face and scowled at her. "It's dumb junk," he muttered.

Crane pulled himself taller. It was the first words he'd heard the boy speak. *I guess it's a good sign.* Though he didn't like the way the boy spoke to Betsy.

Betsy seemed unaffected as she skipped back to Maggie's side and arranged her things in a neat row, humming as she played.

"It's time to get ready for bed," Maggie announced, springing to her feet.

Crane handed Betsy a bedroll. She waited as he flicked his into place, then spread hers beside him. He smiled as he ducked to put more wood on the fire. He carried his coffee to the bedding, where he stretched out, his back to a tree.

Betsy watched him, waiting until he was settled before she crawled under the covers at his side.

"Ted," Maggie called. "Come over here."

Ted's shoulders tightened, and he shifted toward the darkness.

"It's all the bedding we got," she called again. "You'll have to share with us."

His shoulder drew closer to his ear.

Maggie turned toward Crane, her look begging him to do something. He shrugged.

"He'll get cold," Betsy whispered.

Crane nodded. "He's got to make up his own mind."

A heavy, waiting silence settled uneasily around them. Finally, with a sigh from as low as her shoes, Maggie shifted her attention back to the Bible, still lying on her knees. "Do you suppose I could read some?"

Crane nodded. "Go ahead. Read it out loud."

She bent her head and carefully opened the pages to the front and began, " 'In the beginning God created the heaven and the earth.' " Her voice was low and musical.

Crane eased back into a more comfortable position and, beneath his eyelashes, let his gaze skim over the others.

Betsy, her eyes wide and glimmering, a finger wrapped in a corner of the blanket, squirmed around so she could see Maggie.

Maggie's hair fell around her face like a curtain, moving just enough for the golden light to catch in its strands.

As she read, Ted's shoulders relaxed, and he stared at his toes, the light from the fire making sharp angles across his features.

Crane let his gaze return to Maggie. He got the same feeling in his chest he got when Rebel nuzzled his nose against his neck. He let the words take him back to the distant rooms of his memory to a time when they had been a happy family—before Pa left and Ma lost hope. Evenings had a special ritual of their own. Pa settled down before the fire with pipe and coffee. Crane sat on a stool, close enough to lean against Ma's knees. And Ma read aloud from this same Bible.

He drank his cooling coffee. Strange how he had forgotten. Maybe it was why he had kept the Bible; the reason he had put God-fearing as a requirement for his future wife.

Maggie closed the book. "I reckon I better stop for tonight." She sighed deeply. "It's so beautiful. I wish I could read it all right away."

"Me too." Betsy flipped over on her back. "God made everything. Crane," she said, fixing him with a demanding gaze, "Did He make me?"

Crane struggled to find the words to explain how a baby was made. "It took a mamma and papa to make you, Child."

"Of course He did," Maggie interrupted. "My ma always said God made every sparrow and every flower in the grass. He made every one of us. She said little children are the most special so He made an angel for each one to watch over them." She turned to Ted. "You remember that, Ted? You remember our mamma saying that?"

Ted shrugged his back toward them, his narrow shoulders creeping toward his ears.

Maggie ducked her head. Carefully she rewrapped the Bible and returned it to the pack before she crawled in beside Betsy. "Ted, it's getting colder by the minute. Come and lay beside me like we used to do." But Ted didn't respond.

Crane tossed out the last drop of coffee and pushed to his feet. He set the empty cup on a rock, then caught up his heavy gray blanket and wrapped it around Ted's shoulders, ignoring the way the boy stiffened and leaned away. From his saddlebag he pulled out his long black slicker and lay down, huddling under the coat.

"Thank you," Maggie whispered. "I hope you'll be warm enough."

"I'll manage." He'd survived worse.

"You're a nice man," she whispered.

Crane wasn't sure he'd heard her correctly. He grunted and waited until Betsy dug her feet into his ribs before he squirmed into a more comfortable position and waited for his thoughts to quiet.

Out of the darkness a little voice spoke. "I guess his died."

five

He heard Maggie's sharp intake of breath even as his thoughts flared like a hot burst of flame.

"Who died?" Maggie asked, the tension behind her low, calm words ringing in his head.

"Ted's angel," Betsy answered calmly.

"What makes you say that?"

"Well, he was dead or sleeping when your pa sold Ted to that pig man. Otherwise he would have helped Ted."

Smiling, Crane digested the idea, but it wasn't her statement that made him smile; it was the quick way her mind worked, assessing information, evaluating it against her experience, trying to fit it into her world. And he couldn't wait to hear what Maggie would say.

"Far as I know, angels don't die," she muttered. "I don't know about sleeping. Doesn't seem they should need to."

"Then what was he doing?" Betsy demanded. "Maybe playing with someone?"

Crane chuckled deep in his chest. The little minx wasn't going to let it go easily.

Out of the darkness Maggie's voice challenged him. "You like to answer her?"

"No. You're doing fine."

"Thanks." Maggie grunted. "Maybe angels play. Guess I really don't know. But I don't blame the angels or God for what happened to Ted." She paused and drew a trembling breath. "Or me." Another pause. "My ma told me God loved me no matter what. She said He loved me so much He sent His son, Jesus, to die so we could have our sins forgiven and be part of God's family. And she said He would never leave me alone. All I had to do was decide whether I wanted it or not."

Silence descended for a moment.

"If I blame anyone, I blame my pa. Him and his bottle."

Crane stared into the darkness. People did what they did probably not even thinking how it might hurt another. It was useless to blame. It tied you to the past, controlled the present, and pinched the future.

"Best to forget it," he murmured. "What's done is done. We have the rest of our lives ahead of us."

"I suppose you're right. Not much any of us can do about what's already happened. Except learn from it." Her voice hardened. "I know I've learned a few things."

Crane wondered what lessons Maggie had learned, but Betsy snuggled close to his side, her breathing slow and even, and he didn't ask for fear of waking her.

Then out of the darkness Betsy's soft voice asked, "You'll never leave us, will you, Crane?"

It was as much statement as question and drove Crane's breath from him in a gust. "Don't see no reason to." Awkwardly he shifted to one hip so he could drape his arm over Betsy's wee body, letting her know she was safe. He stiffened as his hand touched Maggie's warm fingers. She tensed momentarily, but her hand remained beneath his. Inch by inch he relaxed, letting his hand rest on hers. He liked the warm rush of blood through his veins and wondered what Maggie's reaction would be if he pulled her close. How could he with the child curled between them?

"You never answered her question," Maggie whispered.

"What question?"

"About leaving. Will you ever leave us, Byler Crane?" Her words whispered through the darkness.

"Like I said, I don't see no reason to leave."

"What would constitute a reason?"

He withdrew his hand and threw himself on his back. They were married. Wasn't that promise enough? He said as much.

"Your pa was married, and he left."

He didn't need her pointing it out. His jaw tightened. "I can't answer for my pa, but I recall back in Colhome I promised "til death do us part.' I ain't changed my mind and don't plan to."

She sighed. "That's something, I guess."

"Yup." What more did she want? Theirs wasn't a romantic liaison; it was a business arrangement—one they both stood to benefit from. His parents had married out of love and passion, and look how that turned out. He decided he was more'n happy to do it his way.

"And we'll take care of Ted and Betsy?"

"I ain't about to leave them to fend for themselves." He'd learned to take what life handed him without asking too many questions, but it seemed Maggie wasn't so inclined. "No point in trying to figure out everything. It only boggles you down with worry."

"I'm not trying to figure out everything." She sounded annoyed. "Only where I stand and what I should expect." A minute later she added, "I feel like I've been swept into a whirlwind."

He chuckled. "Mostly of your own making."

"I can't seem to help it."

"I suppose not." Not if she meant to rescue everyone she thought was in trouble.

"I guess I act before I think."

"Umm."

He heard a tiny sigh. "But even if I sat and thought about it a week, I wouldn't put either Betsy or Ted back where they was." Her voice hardened. "It wouldn't be right."

"Nope."

"It's just—" She sounded uncertain. "I only—"

He waited, letting her sort her thoughts.

"You said you needed a God-fearing wife to begin a new life in the West. And now here you are with me and two young'uns. It's not what you bargained for." She took a gusty breath. "I guess what I'm trying to say is, I'd understand if you said you wanted out."

He thought he'd made it clear he was going ahead as

planned. What more did she want? He wriggled away from a lump under his back. He could not promise the future; he could only say, as he already had, he was prepared to continue their journey.

Again he shifted so he could drape his arm over Betsy's sleeping form. Maggie's arm was still there. He found her hand and rested his own on top of it. She curled her fingers away but made no attempt to pull her hand out.

"The past is best left behind, and there's no point in trying to guess what the future might hold. So we make plans as best we can and take each day as it comes."

Her fingers tightened into a ball. "Together?"

He squeezed her hand. "I meant what I said."

The tension in her arm eased. Slowly her fingers uncurled to lay warm and relaxed in his grasp. The child between them snored softly. Maggie's breathing deepened, but he couldn't be certain she slept. Across the fire Ted shifted in his sleep and moaned, the sound choking off as if he'd tied a rope around it.

Crane lay with the child under his arm and Maggie's hand in his. *No promises other than the one I made in front of the preacher. And no assurances.* It was enough to be like this— husband and wife united to face the future. As to the rest of it— His chest tightened so it hurt to breathe. The rest would come later.

The next morning, anxious to be on the trail, Crane silently urged everyone to hurry. Breakfast complete, he left Maggie to clean up as he went to get the horses ready. He was tightening the pack in place when a sound stopped him. He paused to listen. It was a high-pitched keening sound.

Silent as a shadow, he slid between the trees toward the sound. Through the leaves he glimpsed the gurgling water of the river, and as he lifted his gaze to the shoreline, the skin on the back of his neck crawled.

Betsy stood waist-deep in the slow, persistent current, her arms flung out as she struggled to keep her balance. The water caught the too-big shirt she wore, tugging her downstream. Her face was contorted with fear. The keening sound rose from her lips.

Ted stood on the shore facing Betsy, the expression on his face sending shudders across Crane's shoulders. As Crane watched, Ted pitched a rock into the river, splashing water in Betsy's face, forcing her to draw back.

Crane held his breath as she stumbled and righted herself. She took a step toward the shore. Ted threw another rock and forced her back again. The keening sound raced through Crane's veins. Crane's jaw ached from clenching his teeth together. He eased toward the pair, then pulled back as Maggie broke through the trees. She skidded to a stop behind Ted, her hands clenched, her mouth widening. Her gaze flicked from Ted to Betsy, and she took a deep breath.

"Ted, Betsy," she called, as if trying to locate the children. "Where are you? It's about time to leave."

The handful of rocks slipped from Ted's fists, and he plopped down on a boulder, looking detached and disinterested.

Betsy struggled toward shore.

"There you are," Maggie crooned, stepping into the river to help Betsy. "You best be careful around the river. It can be dangerous." She held the child's hand.

Ted studiously avoided looking in their direction.

"We wouldn't want anything to happen." Her voice carried a hard, warning note. "Would we, Ted?"

Slowly he turned toward her. Brother and sister stared at each other. Crane couldn't see Ted's expression, but he could see the set of Maggie's shoulders and the challenge in her face.

Just when he thought Maggie would have to relent, Ted moved his head. It was barely a nod, but Crane sighed.

She smiled grimly. "Then let's get ready to go."

Betsy clung to her hand as they hurried back to the campsite. Ted waited a moment, then jerked to his feet and followed.

His fists clenched at his side, Crane watched until they were out of sight. It was several minutes before he led the horses to the campsite, where Maggie had built up the fire to dry

Betsy's clothes. Crane moved slowly and deliberately, his calm exterior giving no indication of his troubled thoughts. Out of the corner of his eye, he studied Ted, but the boy sat on his former perch, peeling a branch and looking as ordinary as an April shower.

As they rode west, Crane's thoughts knotted, again and again replaying the scene at the river. He barely heard Betsy's chatter or Maggie's replies. He'd have to keep a more careful eye on Ted and wait to see what the boy was made of.

"I recollect the day you was born," Maggie said to Ted. "After you was washed, the midwife wrapped you up and put you in my arms while Ma rested. I remember Pa said, 'I reckon he's going to be as much your baby as anybody's.' " She paused, a faraway look in her eyes. "You were so sweet. You was smiling before you were more'n a few days old. Ma said it was just gas, but Pa watched you and said, 'I declare. He does seem to know when it's Maggie talking to him. There's something special between the two of them.' "

Crane knew what Maggie was doing, trying to bring the boy out of himself and back to the child she remembered. But thinking of the way Ted had treated Betsy, Crane wanted to warn Maggie the brother she once knew might be forever gone.

"Ted," she continued, "Do you remember the time Ma and Pa decided to take us on a picnic down to the river, and Pa made sure you could swim good—then he hung a rope from that big tree and taught us how to swing over the river, and jump in?"

Crane turned to look at Ted where he rode behind his sister. Expecting to see him with head ducked as usual, Crane was startled to see Ted's face lifted to watch Maggie. Crane stared. Perhaps something was redeemable in this child after all.

"Your pa sounds like a right nice man," Betsy said, her voice full of awe.

Maggie nodded. "He was until Ma died, and he took to the bottle. After that he changed." Her voice hardened. "I guess you can never be certain someone won't change from one day to another as they ride down the trail."

Crane sat up straight. He didn't have to look at Maggie to be certain she meant him. But how could he promise her tomorrow and tomorrow? Today was all they could be certain of. Today was all he could promise.

By midafternoon they rode into a town. "We'll get more supplies here," Crane announced, turning in at the general store. Maggie followed. "You all better come in and help get what we need."

The four of them marched up the steps toward the door.

"We need clothes for Betsy. Maggie, you look after that," he said. "I'll see to Ted's needs." He pulled open the door and stepped in.

He selected several blankets and asked for a bag of flour and another of cornmeal before he led Ted to the men's section. He chose three shirts and some overalls, then had Ted sit while they tried on boots. Ted did as he was told without any interest in the proceedings until Crane looked over the pile and said, "I suppose a young fella your age will be needing a pocketknife."

Ted glanced up, giving Crane a chance to see his wide eyes before he ducked his head again. It was long enough for Crane to see a gleam of interest, and he smiled.

"Let's see what they got."

They returned to the counter and asked to see the knives. The storekeep pulled out a tray with eight knives on it and set it before them.

Crane lifted each knife, feeling the weight of it in his palm, then flicking open the blades before he handed it to Ted, who did the same. One by one, they examined each knife, then stared at them lined up on the counter.

"It's your knife—you'll have to decide which is best," Crane said.

He felt Ted's sharp intake of breath, then the boy reached out and picked up a plain black knife with two solid blades.

"Good choice," Crane said, pleased the boy had chosen the sturdiest one rather than going for the flashy red one with all the doodads. "Add this to the tally," he told the storekeep. Ted held it uncertainly in his palm. "It's yours," Crane said. "Carry it in your pocket, and use it wisely."

Ted pushed the knife into the pocket of the new overalls he wore. "Thank you," he murmured, flashing Crane a quick look.

"You're welcome, Boy."

Maggie and Betsy joined them, adding more articles to the pile.

"Look at my new shoes." Betsy pranced before Crane.

"Nice," he said, pleased at how much better she looked in a dress her size. "Looks like we're all set then." He paid the bill. "Now let's go see what we can find for a horse for Ted."

Again the boy flashed him a wide-eyed look. Crane felt compelled to explain himself. "We don't want to overload our mounts and have them wear out before we get where we're going."

Under the watchful but guarded eye of Ted, he purchased a small Morgan gelding and a saddle. Crane was certain Ted sat taller in the saddle as they left town. His glance met Maggie's, and she smiled and mouthed, "Thank you."

He felt heat rush to the tips of his ears. "Let's make tracks." He turned his attention to the trail, his thoughts scattering like the dust at Rebel's hooves. The wind had picked up while they made their purchases, tearing out of the northwest with a hunger that made Crane grab for his coat. Maggie did the same, while he handed the children each a new coat. He'd wanted to ride for three or four hours yet, but after an hour he couldn't abide the misery on the faces of those under his care and pulled in at the first sheltered spot.

"We could be in for a storm." He led them into a stand of trees that cut the wind. "Let's set up camp." Betsy huddled close to a bush while Maggie hunched against the wind. Crane dropped his gaze to Ted, pleased that the boy didn't look away.

"Ted, we'll build a shelter. Maggie and Betsy, you gather up as much wood as you can." He stared at the cloud-darkened sky. "Looks like we might need a good fire tonight."

"Come on, Betsy." The child sniffled as Maggie took her hand.

Crane got his axe and bent thin poplar saplings, cutting them close to the ground, then showed Ted how to weave them into a lean-to. The boy proved a good help despite his shivering.

Crane brushed his hands off. "Think that will do?" he asked Ted.

"Guess so," the boy murmured.

Crane smiled. "Let's get the saddles and bedrolls."

Ted jumped to obey, helping pile the saddles and packs at the edge of the lean-to and shoving the bedrolls into the shelter.

"Come here and get warm," Crane called to Maggie and Betsy, and they hurried inside the shelter.

Ted helped Crane build a fire and stacked wood close by.

"Good boy," Crane murmured. "Now get in out of the cold."

Ted hesitated, looking at the tight quarters, but a cold gust of wind tore through the clearing. The boy crawled in close to the saddles, keeping a space between himself and the others.

Crane had built tree shelters before but always for himself, and although he'd tried to build a larger one this time, only a narrow space was left for him to squirm into. Betsy edged forward to make room for him, resting her elbow against his knee. His left shoulder rubbed against Ted's slight body. Maggie's warmth raced along his other side, and as he shifted, his arm brushed her.

He could hardly breathe. Was she likewise feeling a response to their closeness? Was that why her breathing was so shallow? He wanted to say something, let her know he wanted more from marriage than a physical presence. But he sensed she was as frightened as Ted, and he didn't know how to tell her she didn't need to be afraid of him. Although he wanted a proper marriage, he was willing to bide his time until she was ready.

He hunched over. Betsy's hair tickled his lips as he pulled

items from the saddlebags for supper.

After the meal was cleaned up, Maggie asked, "Would it be hard to get the Bible?"

"No problem at all." He leaned across Ted and lifted it from the pack.

"Would it be all right if I read it again?"

"Yeah, yeah!" Betsy cheered.

"That would be nice," Crane agreed. He shoved more wood into the flames and settled back.

Maggie read story after story. Occasionally, Crane leaned forward to throw on another chunk of wood, and the flames flared, bathing them all in a warm glow.

She read until her voice cracked.

"Guess we should go to sleep," Crane murmured.

She carefully rewrapped the Bible and handed it to him. He tucked it back in the pack.

The children had snuggled down behind them. He was certain Betsy was already sleeping. Maggie tugged her bedroll around between Crane and the children and crawled in. He waited until she was settled, then spread his blankets so he slept across the opening. He lay stiff, afraid his movements would disturb the others.

Betsy kicked a little.

The leaves rustled as Ted shuffled as far away as possible.

Beside him, separated only by the blankets, Maggie lay quiet and still.

Crane filled his lungs slowly and held the air in his chest for a moment, then eased it out through his teeth and forced himself to relax. The night noises settled around him, comforting in their familiarity.

Out of the darkness, Maggie said, "I didn't know I'd forgotten so much."

Crane waited for her to explain.

"All the things my ma told me, the stories she read from the Bible and how she explained about God." She took a deep breath, making her body touch Crane's in several places.

His breathing jerked to a halt.

"I forgot so much. It's like I shoved it all from my mind."

He grunted.

"Guess I let my anger get in the road." She stiffened. "I was so angry when Ted disappeared. And when Pa left me in town, not caring what happened to me. I guess it all made me forget."

He couldn't say much to that and lay still as a deep sigh eased through her. A muffled sound came from Ted's corner, then a barely audible whisper. "Me too."

Maggie wrapped her arms around the boy. "Oh, Ted, I love you so much."

Relief washed through Crane. It was a time of healing for brother and sister. Maggie's words were a faint echo of the things his mother had said to him.

"I let other things get in the road. I don't want you to forget like I did," Maggie said. "I feel like I can hear Ma's voice again."

❧

They hadn't been on the road long the next morning when they saw a tilted wagon. A woman sat on the ground, rocking back and forth. A man stood over her, waving his arms. As they drew closer, Crane heard soft cries from the woman and the deeper tones of the man.

"Now, Marta. It be okay. Somet'ing come off, but we be okay. Now you not cry."

Crane pulled to a stop beside the pair. "Looks like you got problems, Mister."

"Ya, t'at we got. For sure. Dis here wheel come wrong."

Crane dismounted. "Bet you could use a hand fixing it."

"Ya. Dat we can. Dat we can."

The woman on the ground groaned. Her husband turned to watch her. "My missus. . .I t'ink the baby come soon." The man turned imploringly to Crane. "Your missus, she help my missus?"

Crane looked at Maggie. She was so young. And not very big. But she had proven to be spunky. "Can you help?" he murmured.

She grabbed his arm and leaned close. "I ain't never done this before." Her hand slipped down and buried itself in his grasp.

"You never seen a baby born?"

"I seen Ted born."

He squeezed her hand. His heart quickened as she clung to him. "Do what you can."

She looked around. "She needs someplace quiet and clean. A place to lay down."

"Ya. I get 'ta bed off the wagon." And the man jumped into the wagon box, handing Crane a roll of blankets.

Maggie called, "Over here." He took the bedding to her and saw she had found a grassy spot behind some bushes.

"My missus, she have this ready too." The worried man held a satchel toward Maggie. "It have 'ta clean cloths, scissors, and a blanket for the baby."

Maggie returned to the laboring woman. "Can you walk that far?"

"Ya." Marta grunted to her feet and waddled to the spot. Maggie disappeared with her.

Eyes big, Betsy and Ted stared after them, Betsy plucking at the hem of her dress. Ted's arms hung stiff and straight at his side.

"Come on, you two," Crane called. "I need some help." He handed the reins to Ted. "Hold the horses while I have a look." He crawled under the wagon. The axle was cracked. He eased out and spoke to the man. "You got a spare axle, Mr.—? Sorry, I don't know your name."

"I ban Mr. Swedburg." He held out his hand. Crane introduced his group.

"I not got spare axle."

"Then we'll have to patch the old one. You'll have to go back to town and get it done proper."

"Ya."

"Now let's see if we can get the wheel back on."

But when Crane put his back to the wagon, it would not

budge. He checked inside and saw a stove, a trunk, and several boxes piled in the corner. "We'll need to move some of this stuff."

Swedburg disappeared in the back of the wagon and returned with a basket. "We better move Mamma and her babies first. Maybe the little girl like to play with dem."

The basket held a purring cat with four half-grown nursing kittens. "Betsy, you want to look after this bunch while we fix the wagon?" Crane placed the basket on the grass out of harm's way, grinning as Betsy bent over to pet the kittens.

He and Ted helped the man rearrange the contents of the wagon, distributing the heavy objects away from the broken wheel. "Be careful not to put all your big things over one wheel," Crane told Swedburg.

"I not t'ink very good. I just t'ink about getting free land. I want to get dere before baby born." He paused and listened to his wife's moans. "I t'ink it be too late now."

"Now there'll be another reason to get there."

Crane showed him how to grease the wheel and reinforce the axle. "Now there are three of you. You're a family." Even as he had gone from being alone to a family of four. The thought made him feel warm inside. And at the same time, a little apprehensive. It was an awesome responsibility for one who had spent his life alone.

"Ya. We start new life." The man smiled at Crane. "You too, ya?"

Stepping back from the repair job, Crane nodded and wiped his hands on a rag. "It should get you back to town."

"I t'ank you."

Whatever reply Crane had thought to make was drowned by a scream that ripped through his brain. Swedburg's face blanched. For a moment Crane thought the man would faint; then the color seeped back into his face.

"Da little one not want to come, maybe."

Crane pushed his hat back. "I'm sure everything's all right."

six

The children each held a kitten, but Crane could sense their fear as they turned to him.

"I'm sure everything is fine," he said again, ignoring the shiver racing up his spine. He turned to Swedburg. "Let's get the wagon repacked."

But the man let Crane do most of the work of putting crates along the wall.

"Mr. Swedburg," Maggie called, and the man rubbed his hands on his pants and looked toward the bushes, then back at Crane. "You have a son!" Maggie's voice sang out as she stepped into sight, a small, blanketed bundle in her arms.

The baby wailed as Maggie placed him in his father's arms. "Congratulations."

"Marta?"

"She's fine. Resting for a few minutes."

Crane dropped his hand to her shoulder and squeezed. "Good job," he murmured. Feeling her trembling, he pulled her close. She almost collapsed against him.

After a moment she straightened. "I'd best go take care of Marta." And she slipped away, leaving an empty coldness at Crane's side.

They stayed long enough to get Marta settled in the wagon with the infant at her side.

"Now we must put the cat back."

But Swedburg looked from the basket to the two children. "Ve have too many cats. You take one, ya? Let the children choose."

Two pairs of begging eyes turned to Crane.

"A cat is good when you build new house. Keep the mices out. Ya?"

"Please, Crane. Please," Betsy begged. "We'll take good care of it, won't we, Ted?" She looked to Ted for confirmation.

Ted nodded.

But it was not Betsy's eager pleading that convinced Crane; it was the resigned look in the boy's eyes that said he expected to be denied.

"You two will have to agree which one you want."

Betsy whooped her delight, but Crane's reward was Ted's wide grin before he turned back to the cats.

Betsy lined them up, petting each. "I like them all."

"We can only take one," Crane warned.

"I know," she whispered.

Maggie joined the children. "They're adorable. How will you decide which one to take?"

"I can't," Betsy wailed, turning to Ted. "You choose."

Ted had been sitting back, watching, and now he nodded and began to draw little circles on the knee of his pants.

The others watched quietly.

"What we want is a kitty that is alert. One that's smart enough to know what's going on," Ted said.

Crane narrowed his eyes and studied the boy. It was difficult to see this lad as the same one who had tormented Betsy not much more than a day ago. But he'd sensed a difference in the boy all morning. The stiffness was gone. And the guarded fear. Crane chewed his bottom lip. Seems a door had been broken down last night. Whether it was the memories sparked by Maggie reading the Bible or her talk about their ma, he didn't know, and it didn't matter. He only hoped the boy could leave the past behind and get on with the future.

A gray-striped kitten detached itself from the others, tail lifted like a flag, and stalked toward the circling finger. It sprang to Ted's knee, grasping the finger in its paws. Ted laughed, tickling the kitten's tummy. He played with the animal a minute, then cradled him to his face. The kitten licked Ted's cheek. Crane could hear the cat purring even where he stood.

"That the one, Ted?" Maggie asked.

The boy nodded.

"Here's a blanket for him." Swedburg handed a scrap of gray material to Ted. "You wrap him up, and he travel good."

Ted bundled the kitten up and rose to his feet. He held the bundle out to Betsy. "We'll take turns carrying him. You go first."

Amidst a flurry of thank-yous and good-byes, Crane, Maggie, and the children again headed west.

෨

It was two afternoons later as Crane returned from hunting that he heard high-pitched squealing and the sound of splashing water. He angled toward the river and saw Maggie and the children playing in the water. Ted was several feet from Maggie, and he sang a little tune, "Baggy Maggie, you're so shaggy. Raggy, raggy, raggy." He laughed.

Maggie swept her cupped hand through the water, spraying an arc of water in Ted's face.

Crane's gaze lingered on Maggie as she laughed. She had stripped down to some sort of lace-trimmed undergarment rounded at the neck. Her arms were bare. Gems of water glistened on her skin.

Ted continued his teasing. "Raggy, baggy, shaggy Maggie."

Betsy joined the chorus, jumping up and down in the water. "Baggy Maggie, baggy Maggie."

She sprayed them both with water, calling, "Ted, Ted, your head is red. Ted, Ted, go to bed." She turned to Betsy. "Miss Betsy, you're so pesky."

Then she saw Crane watching them, and her words sputtered to a halt. She sank into the water. "We were just playing," she muttered, her gaze never leaving his face.

He took a step closer, drawn by an indescribable force.

"Come in the water," Betsy called. "It's lots of fun."

Crane shook his head and stepped back. Maggie's gaze dropped but not before Crane caught a flash in her blue eyes.

Was it a wish for their relationship to progress to the next step, or was it simply the reflection of the sunlight off the water?

The children flung water at him, and he ducked away, catching his hat on a branch, tipping it over his forehead. As he pushed it back, his gaze returned to Maggie. He knew what he wanted. He wanted to be man and wife in more than name. He ached to hold her to his chest and kiss her lips, red and moist from playing in the river.

"Come on," Betsy called again.

Crane considered the idea, half deciding to join them, then thought better of it. He might know what he wanted, but he had no notion what Maggie was feeling. He could afford to be patient. He'd let Maggie find her own way in her own time. They had the rest of their lives.

"I got us a rabbit. Best get it roasting." And he walked away, feeling strangely hollow inside. And it wasn't from hunger.

By the time the others joined him, he sat on the ground tending the rabbit on a spit over the fire and, looking up, caught Maggie watching him, her eyes wide and steady. She held his gaze for a moment before turning her attention to the cup of coffee in her hand.

He reached around Betsy to turn the meat. His own words condemned him. *No love or passion,* he'd told himself. But now he wanted both. He longed for physical closeness, but even more, a place deep inside him ached for her love.

He set Betsy aside and pushed to his feet. "I'm going to see what Ted's up to." He stalked into the dusk.

Ted wasn't difficult to locate. He sat near the river's edge, holding the kitten, which the children had named Cat, and staring into the distance. Although Ted had changed dramatically in the passing days, Crane noticed he often sought solitude. He crossed to Ted's side and sat beside him.

The silence settled around them, broken only by Cat's purring and the murmur of the river. They had no need for words. Sometimes a man had to work things out inside himself. He was sure it was as true for Ted as for him.

"Crane, Ted." Betsy raced toward them. "Maggie says it's ready to eat."

"Better not keep Betsy waiting," Crane murmured out of the side of his mouth. "She'll think she'll starve if we do."

Ted rewarded him with a flash of a smile. "Bet she's been pestering Maggie steady, wanting to know if it was ready."

Crane chuckled as he scrambled to his feet. "Nothing quite so important as food, is there?"

Seemed Ted liked his food almost as well as Betsy, but Crane wasn't about to point it out.

"Not so far as Betsy knows." Ted followed Crane toward the fire. "It's hard being hungry." His voice was thoughtful. "But there are harder things."

Crane wanted to ask what the other things were, but Betsy tugged on his hand, chattering like a magpie as she hurried him along.

Later, having eaten their fill, the children played with Cat, tossing a knob of wood back and forth between them, getting her to chase it.

Maggie brought the coffeepot and refilled his cup. She set the pot back and sank to the ground, her face upturned to him. "I've been thinking."

He had been about to take a swallow, but at her words, his throat tightened and he lowered his cup.

"I think I should write Pa and tell him I got Ted. And when we get settled, I'll let him know where we are."

The coffee sloshed in Crane's cup. "You think he might want Ted?" He watched the boy playing with Betsy. He was quiet compared to the girl, but underneath the scars left by the hands of the pig farmer, Ted seemed to be a nice boy. Crane's fist tightened around his cup, and he admitted he had grown fond of him.

"I wouldn't think so. He knows I'll take good care of him. But maybe someday he'll put his bottle down and remember how much he cared about us. Maybe he'll wonder how we're doing."

Crane's gaze shifted to Betsy. "Will someone claim Betsy one day?"

"I thought about it some." Maggie's face caught the flare of the fire, making her eyes bright. Her moods flashed across her face as quick as the light from the fire. She was open and direct. If she wanted a change in their relationship, she would come right out and say so. But she hadn't.

She looked at him steadily, and he forced his thoughts back to the conversation. "Ma knew someone who had a foundling child. She said the lady got a lawyer to make some inquiries, and when no one turned up, she adopted the child, legallike. Maybe we should do that too."

He nodded. "Soon as we find a place to settle, we'll contact a lawyer."

She smiled. "It's funny, don't you think? All of us have lost our families, and now here we are together. A new family." Her expression flattened; her voice grew harsh. "A forever family."

Crane stared into the fire. Was there such a thing as forever?

Taking his silence for disagreement, she shifted her back to him. "I know we can't see what the future holds." Her voice was low. "But we can promise ourselves and each other that as far as possible, as much as lies within our power, we won't change our minds."

Until death do us part. He'd promised it when they wed; he'd reiterated it since, but she wanted more. Trouble was, he didn't know what it was or if he could give it. "What is it you want me to say?"

For a moment she didn't reply. Then she shrugged. "I don't know. It's just—" She hesitated. "I no longer believe in happy ever after." Her voice dropped to a whisper. "But I want to." She lifted her head again. "I want to believe we will ride west and find a place we like and build a new home where we will be a true family." She rubbed her clenched hand against her knee. "But I'm afraid when we get to the end of the trail, it will all fall apart."

Crane reached out and squeezed her shoulder. For a spell he was silent, then he said, "A man is only as good as his word." Beneath his hand her shoulder slumped. His answer had disappointed her, but he didn't know what else to say. Seemed some people could make promises easily. And forget them as easily. He had no wish to be one of those men.

He rose and called the children, handing them each a bedroll. "Time to settle in."

Betsy spread her blankets next to his as always. Maggie unrolled her blankets on the other side of the child. Ted waited until the others were finished, then flipped his bedroll next to Maggie's.

Crane poured himself and Maggie another cup of coffee and handed her the Bible. He lounged on his bed, sipping his coffee, but she hadn't read long when her voice thickened, and she choked. Tears washed her face, and she dashed them away.

"My ma told me I could be a child of God. He loved me enough to send His Son, Jesus, so I could be forgiven. All I had to do was ask. And I did." She sniffed. "She said He would always be my father, no matter what happened to me." Again she sniffed and took a long, shuddering breath. "How could I forget so much?"

The children watched her—Ted's face pinched, Betsy's eyes big, and her mouth round.

Maggie jerked around to face them all. "Ted, Betsy, Crane, listen to me. We can each be a child of God. He will always take care of us. It doesn't matter where we go or who tries to hurt us—God will love us forever."

Although her fervor made him squirm, Crane couldn't turn away from the dark gleam in her eyes.

"Ma said we could never for sure count on men, but we can always count on God."

Crane clenched his mug, certain her comment held a note of censure. But then he could hardly fault her if she held no confidence in men. Her experiences had not given her cause.

It would take time for him to prove himself.

She leaned toward the children. "I know bad things happened to you. They happened to us all, but God will help us. From now on I'm going to trust God to take care of me. He promised He would. Forever."

Crane leaned back, staring at the stars. His own mother had said much the same thing the last visit he'd had.

"I've failed to prepare you for the future the way I should," she'd said. He could still feel her frail hand clasping at his arm. "Remember—no matter how your pa and I have failed, God never changes. He is the same forever."

He scrubbed a hand over his face. He simply couldn't believe in forever. Seemed like a man was better off doing his best and letting the future take care of itself.

❧

The next morning, Maggie sang loudly as she worked. Betsy laughed, and soon they both sang.

Ted wore a longing expression. He turned toward Crane, and the moment their eyes met, Crane knew Ted wasn't ready to trust anyone. Or anything.

"Come on, Ted," he murmured. "Let's get the horses ready."

Ted leapt to do his bidding. He had proven to be a quick learner and worked efficiently at Crane's side. Neither of them spoke until they were cinching the saddles.

"What'd you think about that stuff?" Ted asked, his words muffled as he reached under his gelding.

"What stuff?" Crane stalled.

"The stuff Maggie says about God." Ted straightened to look directly at Crane. "About being able to go to heaven and all that."

Crane secured the pack on the spare horse before he answered. "Well, I reckon it must all be true. It's in the Bible, isn't it?"

"But what do you think about it?" He pinned Crane with his question. The boy deserved honesty.

"I guess it's hard to separate out things. Things people do

get mixed up with what God says. Seems like they should be closer together."

"Yeah, know what you mean."

"Don't mean it's not true. Don't mean I don't believe it. It's just real hard to sort it out. I need to do some heavy thinking on it."

But it seemed thinking wasn't something Maggie was prepared to let him do. As soon as they hit the trail, she started talking. "It's your mother's Bible. She'd underlined lots of verses. She must have known this."

"I reckon she did."

"She tell you about it?"

"Yup. I reckon."

"Well, my ma said it was a gift, but a gift don't do you no good if you don't take it."

"I reckon that's so." He was beginning to wish they'd run into the Swedburgs again, if only because it would give them something else to talk about.

The cat lay curled in Ted's lap. Cat had turned out to be a good traveler, content to spend hours on the saddle. And now, when Crane longed for a diversion, she slept as if life held nothing else.

"I know," Maggie continued. "You're afraid."

Crane interrupted before she could finish. "Men have been shot for saying that," he growled.

"Crane ain't afraid," Ted yelled. "He needs time to think."

She waved little circles with her hands. "I don't mean afraid of somebody or something. I mean afraid to let go and trust."

"Maggie's right," Betsy insisted. "I did what she said. I prayed like she said. She's right."

Ted looked at Crane and said, "We need time to think about it. Don't we, Crane?"

Crane shifted in his saddle and stared dead ahead. It was two against two, a divided camp—a situation that made his nerves crackle. He turned to Maggie. "You was the one who didn't want nothing to change."

Her smile faded, and her face tightened. "Nothing's changed. We're still headed west, ain't we?"

Their gazes locked. Neither of them shifted away. Finally he grunted and kicked his horse into a trot.

After a few minutes he allowed them to settle into a steady walk.

"Crane?" Betsy's voice was thin.

"Yup."

"You mad at Maggie?"

"Mad?" Had she taken his silence for anger? "No, I was just thinking." Though for the life of him, he couldn't recall one thought.

"Good." Her voice rose, and she began to chatter to Maggie about Cat and birds and asked what they would have for lunch.

Crane grinned at Maggie.

"I 'spect we'll find something," she muttered with an exasperated glance heavenward.

They made good progress that day. As they pulled up to make camp, Crane said, "We're in the Territories now. Tomorrow we'll leave off following the river and drop down to the new rail line." He'd heard the travel was easy with settlements along the new tracks. And although he had no interest in the towns, he understood it was the fastest route to the new West.

With camp set up, Ted wandered down to the river. Crane watched him. All day he'd felt the boy's withdrawal and knew he needed to be alone to sort things out. But the meal was ready, and Ted had not returned.

Maggie called him again, then hurried down to the water's edge. "Ted," she called and waited. But Ted did not answer. She hurried back to the fire, twisting her hands together. "He should have been back."

Crane nodded. "Yup. I was thinking the same." He pushed to his feet. "I'll go get him."

He followed the river, occasionally seeing Ted's track in the soft ground. He walked for the better part of a half hour with no sign of the boy. The muscles in the back of his neck tensed. The boy couldn't have disappeared into thin air. He searched the now rocky ground and found no tracks, but as he edged his way around some willow branches, he sucked in his breath. Ted floated in the river, bobbing with the current.

Crane's thoughts crashed like a wave. A groan rose from deep inside him. Then Ted turned toward him, and Crane saw the muddied streaks down his cheeks and his quivering lips, and he leapt forward.

Ted saw him. "Crane, help." His words rattled over his teeth. "I'm stuck."

"I'm coming. Hang on!" He ran into the water, grabbing the boy under his arms. But he couldn't lift him.

"It's my foot." Ted choked back a sob.

"It'll be all right." Crane swooped his hand down the boy's leg and found it wedged between two boulders. A trickle of pink fled downstream from his foot.

Crane wrapped his arms around one rock and heaved. But it refused to budge. "I'll get something to pry with."

He plowed his way through the water and ran to the trees. The closer trees were willows with only thin whips for branches. He had to find a sturdy branch.

He pushed through to the heavier growth and grabbed the first sizable branch he saw, racing back to the river. Grunting, he pried the end under the boulder and heaved, bending the branch with his weight. He grunted and pushed again. The branch snapped, but the rock did not move.

"I'm gonna have to force your foot out."

The boy nodded, gritting his teeth. "I can take it."

Crane bent over, feeling underwater, locating the best angle to free the foot. If he twisted and pulled at the same time—it would hurt like fury, but he had run out of ideas.

"Hold on now." He shut his mind to the pain he was about to inflict. "Take a deep breath and hold it." He grasped the foot with both hands and pulled. It stuck. He continued to pull, and it came free with a sickening jerk. Ted's scream tore through his brain.

He grabbed the boy, crushing him to his chest, and plunged out of the cold water. "Are you all right?" He held the boy a moment, then set him down and looked deep into his eyes.

Ted nodded, then Crane bent to check the foot. A nasty gash bled profusely, but the foot and ankle seemed otherwise sound.

Ted's teeth chattered. "I was so scared," he whispered.

At the look of misery on his face, Crane pulled the boy back into his arms and held him tight. He wanted to say something to comfort and soothe the boy, but no words came. He pressed the small head against his chest and held him, letting his own fears slip away.

"You're freezing. Slip out of those wet things."

But Ted's fingers were clumsy from the cold, and it was Crane who undid the buttons and pulled the clothes off. With nothing dry to wrap him in, Crane stripped off his water-blotched shirt and wrapped it around Ted. He wrung as much water as he could from Ted's wet clothes, then tied them in a bundle and hooked it to the back loop of his pants.

"Let's get you back to camp." And he swept the boy into his arms. Ted allowed himself to be carried, clinging to Crane as if he feared he was still drowning. They could see the fire ahead and Maggie peering into the darkness.

"I found him!" Crane called.

Maggie raced toward Ted. "He's hurt!" she cried as she saw Ted in Crane's arms. "Oh, Baby, say something."

"It's just my foot." Ted's voice quavered. "I slipped and caught it between two rocks."

Maggie reached for Ted, but Crane shook his head. "Get some blankets ready. He's cold."

She sped to the bedrolls, yanking up the blankets and racing back.

At the fire Crane lowered Ted to the ground. Maggie had the blankets around him before Crane finished pulling away the damp shirt. She grabbed the shirt and saw the blood on it. "He's hurt." Her gaze settled on his foot, and she bent to examine it.

"It's a nasty cut."

"It's clean." Crane put on a fresh shirt. "Right now we need to get him warmed up."

"I made some tea." She hurried to get a cupful, ladling in several spoonfuls of sugar. "Here, sip this." She held it to the boy's mouth.

"Is he all right?" Betsy whispered.

Crane turned to the child. She stood apart from them, pinching the seams of her dress.

"He'll be just fine. He's cold now, and he has a cut on his foot." He reached for her, and she sprang into his arms, burrowing against his chest.

"I didn't want anything to happen to him."

"I know," he said softly. "None of us did."

"I asked God to help you find him." She snuggled closer, relaxing in his arms. "I guess He did."

"Maybe He did at that." Crane was grateful for whatever help God had offered.

Maggie brought some material from her pack and tore it into strips, bandaging Ted's foot.

"Here, Cat," Betsy called the animal to her. "You come keep Ted warm." She parked Cat in Ted's lap.

"Thanks," he whispered.

Crane and Maggie smiled at each other. Crane wondered if she was thinking the same as he: These two have come a long way.

Betsy climbed back into Crane's lap. Suddenly she cried out.

"What's the matter?" Crane asked.

"Your hands." She pointed, tears welling up in her eyes. "They're hurt."

Crane looked at his hands. Blood dripped from the backs of both of them. "I must have cut them pulling Ted's foot out." Strange, he never felt a thing. He was about to wipe his hands on his shirt when Maggie grabbed them.

"Here—let me clean them."

His hand rested in her palm as she wiped the back with a damp cloth, then wrapped his hand in clean rags. Her touch was gentle as the warm summer rain, warming him all over. He shivered, not from cold but from some unfamiliar longing flooding through him.

She looked up from her task. "You're cold," she muttered. "You should take better care of yourself." She turned to the child. "Betsy, get Crane a blanket."

The girl ran to do as she was told, tenderly wrapping the blanket around Crane, patting his shoulders. He wasn't cold; yet their touches calmed his insides better than a hot drink.

They finally got around to having their supper.

Crane kept a close eye on Ted, but he seemed none the worse for his accident. He sat close to the fire, laughing at Cat's antics. In fact, Crane decided, Betsy seemed more affected by the incident than Ted. She hovered at his side, trying to anticipate his needs and satisfy them.

Maggie, having finished her chores, wandered down to the river. Crane watched her from his spot near the fire and, seeing the children were playing happily, sauntered down to join her. He knew she was aware of his presence, but she stared out across the water without speaking.

After awhile, she let out a shuddering breath. "Thank you. You saved his life. I can never thank you enough."

"It was nothing," he murmured.

"I don't know what I would do if anything happened to Ted."

He kept his gaze on the trees across the stream. There she was wanting assurances about the future again. He couldn't promise her nothing would ever happen to Ted. He couldn't promise that for himself. Not for anybody.

"Ted kept his head."

"Poor boy." She swallowed a little cry. "Oh, Crane. He must have been so scared. I was so scared." And she flung herself against his chest, almost toppling him over.

seven

Crane wrapped his arms around her, promising himself he would do his best to see nothing ever hurt her. He rubbed her back, feeling her leanness, her toughness, and her softness.

"Everything will be fine," he murmured.

No sooner had he spoken the words than he wished for them back. He couldn't be making promises he didn't know if he could keep. The feel of her in his arms had turned his mind to mush.

He cupped a hand over her hair. It was so silky. Like nothing he could remember feeling before. He lowered his head, letting his lips caress her hair. He was drowning in the scent of her, the feel of her, the pound of his heart against her slight form.

"God took care of us today," she murmured, her voice muffled against his chest.

Her breath was sweet and tempting, and he lowered his head a fraction more, willing her to lift her face and offer her lips.

Instead she pushed away.

Crane's hands lingered on her waist until she dropped to her knees. He crossed his arms, striving to still the wild emotions raging inside him. She knelt beside him, her hands clasped before her. "Thank You, God, for taking care of Ted today. Thank You for sending Crane to help him." She paused. "Thank You for sending Crane to help us all."

He squirmed. *She must think I'm was something I'm not.* Yet it made him think of something his mother used to say when he did something she appreciated.

"Why, bless you, Byler," she'd say. That was the feeling he got listening to Maggie thank God for him. A sense of being blessed.

Maggie got to her feet and stood close to him. A flash

from the fire threw sharp angles across her face, then her features disappeared in the darkness.

He could feel her breath against his chin. She was watching him. But he didn't know what she wanted. Then she grabbed his hand, sending a wave of warmth up his arm.

"Let's go have coffee." He could hear the smile in her voice.

Her hand felt small and soft, and he let her pull him toward the fire, a smug smile widening his mouth.

They stepped into the circle of light, and she dropped hold of his hand, rushing toward the coffeepot. His arms hung at his sides, and his stare followed her movements. Had their touching affected her the same way it did him?

After they'd settled the children in bed, Crane handed Maggie the Bible. Betsy leaned across his legs, her focus on Maggie, while Ted sat cross-legged at his other side.

Maggie began to read, but her voice faded before she finished the story. Crane watched over his lowered cup. Her thoughts seemed to be far away as she stared at the fire, then slowly closed the book.

"I can't read tonight," she murmured. "My thoughts are too full." The golden light danced across her face. "Seems like a door in my mind has come open, and I can remember all kinds of stuff. Things Ma used to tell me." She turned quickly, fixing her gaze on Ted. "Ted, I don't know what you remember. Seems you weren't very old when Ma started feeling poorly."

Ted's gaze fastened on his sister's face. "I don't remember much."

She nodded. "Sometimes she could barely get out of bed. It was an effort just to talk, but she was always so kind and gentle. I don't ever remember her bein' cross even when Pa was angry with her." Maggie paused to brush an insect from her arm. "I used to think he was angry at her for being sick, but I guess maybe he was angry at the sickness for what it was doing to her." She looked deep into Ted's eyes. "You remember that?"

He shook his head. "I only remember Pa bein' mad."

A flash of pain crossed her face. "You missed the best years."

Maggie leaned back, a gentle smile on her lips. "Ma used to tell the best stories. Stories from the Bible, but lots of stories about her life too."

Betsy shifted toward Maggie, her elbow digging into Crane's leg, but he welcomed the feel of her against him.

"She told about going to church in the old country."

Betsy's head jerked up. "What's church?"

Maggie laughed low in her throat. "It's where you go to worship God and learn about Him."

"How do you do that?" the child demanded.

"You sing songs about God, you read from the Bible and talk about what it means, and someone prays."

Betsy eased back down. "Sounds good."

"Ma told one story over and over about how she heard what she called 'the truth about God.' " She leaned over her knees, a soft expression on her face. "There was a roving preacher who walked about the country with nothing but an old bag holding a change of clothes and his Bible. He'd sit in the center of town and begin to talk, and soon a crowd would be gathered." Maggie chuckled. "Ma said he'd gather a crowd, then preach them into the kingdom."

Crane lay back against the tree trunk maintaining a casual pose, but inside he was hanging on to every word as eagerly as the children.

"How'd he do that?" Betsy asked.

"Ma said he opened his Bible and read verse after verse, telling the people God had given them a gift of salvation. We didn't need to work for it or pay for it. Then he offered a coin to anyone who would come and take it. Ma said only one little boy had the nerve to go up and take it. Then the preacher said, 'That's exactly how it is with God's gift. You just have to take it.'" Her voice drifted off, and Crane could see she was deep in thought.

Betsy sighed. "I wish I'd been there to get the coin."

Maggie fixed her gaze on Betsy. "But don't you see what he was trying to do?"

Betsy shook her head.

"After the little boy got the coin, a bunch crowded around him saying they wished they'd gone and taken it. But what God offers is so much more than a coin. And all we have to do is take it. 'A gift beyond compare,' Ma always said. It's for everyone who decides to become a child of God."

Betsy sat up. "Then I got the gift?"

Maggie laughed. "You do indeed."

Betsy flopped down on her back. "Ain't I happy?"

Later that night, the four of them stretched out side by side. Crane looked up at the stars, his thoughts going round and round on what Maggie had said. Words he was sure his mother would have agreed with. But he couldn't just take a gift. Not from anyone and certainly not from God. He had learned a long time ago to stand strong and alone. Somehow, to take a gift made him beholden to the giver. But that didn't make sense in God's case. After all, didn't he believe God had a hand in the events of people's lives? Then he already was beholden in some fashion. Or was he protected and blessed?

It made his head ache trying to sort it out, so he turned his thoughts toward another matter: Maggie.

At that moment Maggie sat up. "Crane, you sleeping?"

"No," he whispered.

"I want to thank you properly for rescuing Ted."

"You already did." Had she forgotten or—a little pulse thumped inside his head—did she have something more than words in mind?

She flopped down on her back. "I guess I did, but I want to be certain you know how grateful I am."

"I do."

She reached across Betsy's sleeping form, found his hand, and squeezed it. Crane thought his heart would explode at her touch. It was all he could do to lie there when every inch of his body ached to pull her into his arms and cradle her close.

"I care about the boy too," he muttered, his tongue feeling as if he'd been on a long trail ride without a canteen.

"I know you do. You take good care of us all."

"Yup." His mind refused to work.

She lay there, silently holding his hand; then, sighing, she pulled away. "I wanted you to know."

&

The sun poured down on them day after day. What energy the sun didn't soak up, the wind blew away. The grass on the prairie was as high as the horses' bellies, but it was a lone, echoing place with no appeal for him.

"The wind sucks at my soul," Maggie shuddered. "I wouldn't want to live out in the open like this."

Crane nodded. They would continue west until they crossed the wide stretch of flatland. "West of Calgary we'll find trees and foothills," he said.

"I can hardly wait." She rubbed a rag across the back of her neck. "This heat is about more'n I can bear."

"Can't we stop?" Betsy whined.

Ted answered before Crane could. "You see a place where it's gonna be any cooler?"

"We'll stop early tonight," Crane promised.

The heat had taken its toll on everyone. Only Cat, curled up on the saddle in front of Ted, seemed unaffected.

"Maybe we'll find someplace close to water so we can take a dip." Not for the first time he regretted leaving the river.

They rode another hour without seeing anything big enough to squat beside, let alone provide shelter from the sun. Finally, shading his eyes against the glare, he saw a structure against the sky. "There's a water tower ahead."

Water had taken a role the size of the wide sky as they crossed this barren land. The heat waves shimmered along the horizon. Dust wrapped around the wooden tower. A train came toward them, belching and snorting as it slowed.

"Take it easy," he ordered Rebel as he reined in and dismounted.

The others watched Crane with languid interest as he reached toward the spout. He was about to release the water when the engineer blew the whistle. It shuddered down Crane's spine.

Rebel took off as if he'd been shot, Betsy clinging to his back.

"You jughead!" Crane shouted. "Get back here!"

He had his hands full holding the packhorse. Maggie struggled to keep Liberty under control. Cat yowled and scampered up the side of the water tower.

The little Morgan Ted rode seemed to be the only horse with any sense in his head. He sidestepped twice. His nostrils flared, but he didn't bolt. Before Crane could react, Ted kicked his horse into a run and took off after Betsy.

Crane stared after Ted. "He ain't got a chance. No way that old horse is gonna catch Rebel."

Maggie dropped from her mount and grabbed the reins of the packhorse. "Take Liberty!" she cried. "Catch them before someone gets hurt."

Crane leapt into the saddle, reining the horse after the pair, though he was doubtful he could catch them. Betsy bounced madly on Rebel's back, her hair flying out like a spray of yellow straw.

"Hang on!" Crane called, knowing she couldn't hear him.

Ted bent low over the saddle, going for all he was worth, but he wasn't gaining on them. Behind him the train screeched to a stop, and steam whistled out. Liberty jumped sideways.

"Settle down, you knothead," Crane growled. "We got things to do." He struggled with the horse a few minutes, muttering under his breath.

But he could see Rebel was slowing down. Rebel didn't often act so silly and was probably beginning to feel a bit foolish about now.

Ted drew abreast of the bigger horse and caught the reins. Both horses stopped, their sides heaving. By the time Crane caught up, Betsy had crawled off Rebel's back and into Ted's arms, sobbing against his chest. Ted had his arms around the girl, an expression of mingled shock and awe on his face.

Crane grabbed Rebel's reins. "Betsy, are you okay?"

"Yes," she sobbed. "Ted saved me."

"Come on—I'll give you a ride back."

She shook her head, clinging to Ted.

"It's okay," Ted murmured.

They plodded back to the water tower where the train crew had joined Maggie. One man stepped toward Crane. "I'm sorry. I didn't mean to cause you a problem."

"No harm done."

Maggie rushed to the children. "Are you all right?" Betsy fell into Maggie's arms, sobbing. "Shh. Shh." She reached out and patted Ted's knee. "I'm real proud of you, Ted."

Crane waited until the boy got down to put his hand on his shoulder and say in a low tone, "You did a right fine job, Son."

If they hadn't been so desperate for water, they would have left the place; but surrounded by curious, apologetic men, they led the horses to the trough. Maggie insisted the children strip to their undergarments and allow her to splash them with the tepid water. Then they filled the canteens and prepared to leave.

"You folks looking for a place to camp?" the engineer asked.

"Yup." Crane secured the last canteen.

"Ride north." He pointed across the flat prairie. "There's a nice grove of trees. Good camping spot."

"Thanks." Crane reached for Betsy, but she stepped away.

"I want to ride with Ted."

Crane raised his eyebrows, but Ted nodded. Betsy grinned widely as she sat in the saddle, Ted's arms around her as he took the reins.

They found the spot the man had told them about. The poplars were thin but tall enough to shade them from the lowering sun.

The children got their bedrolls shortly after supper and spread them out, Betsy's next to Crane's as always. But when

Ted started to spread his on the other side of Maggie's, Betsy said, "No. You sleep here," pointing to a spot between Maggie and her.

Crane watched the pair, waiting to see how Ted would respond.

The boy hesitated, looking at the spot he'd chosen, then at the place Betsy indicated. The bedroll draped from his arm. He didn't move.

"Please, Ted. I want you to." Betsy sounded as if she would cry any moment, and the boy flipped his blankets open where she pointed. A deep sigh shook her small frame, and smiling her satisfaction, she sat down on her blankets, petting Cat. "You can read now, Maggie."

Crane laughed. The little minx had a way of binding people close to her, then basking in their closeness. She'd succeeded in drawing Ted into her circle.

Maggie grinned at him. He held her gaze until her cheeks darkened, and she lowered her eyes. He kept hoping they would find a way of getting closer. Instead, the children succeeded in pushing them farther apart. He supposed he should be grateful she hadn't found half a dozen waifs to rescue.

He rubbed his chin. Someday he and Maggie were simply gonna have to talk.

❧

It was ten o'clock before the sun dipped behind the horizon, but the heat refused to abate. The children had fallen into a restless sleep, but Crane found it too hot and his mind too active as he tried to sort out his feelings.

He was drawn to Maggie in a way that took his breath away. He hadn't expected this sort of reaction. A "godly woman" to help build a new home, he'd decided, never clearly seeing in his mind where it could lead.

He stared at the star-studded sky. In his schemes the woman had been a silent, shadowy figure—he grinned up at the sky— not this fireball. He ached to tame her. No, he amended, he didn't want to tame her; he loved the spit and fire of her. He only wanted some of that passion turned toward him. His hungry hollowness tore at his gut.

Purposely he turned his thoughts toward the things she'd said about God's love and trusting Him to receive the gift of salvation. She made it all sound so easy, but it didn't feel easy to him. Was his pride getting in the way? But he'd never considered himself a prideful man.

Fear, Maggie had said. But what was there to be afraid of? He wasn't afraid of God.

He was desperate for coffee and pushed to his feet.

"Something the matter?" Maggie called.

"Think I'll build a small fire. I want coffee."

She rolled off her blanket. "Too hot to sleep, isn't it?" She waited as he put the coffee to brew.

He could feel a tension in her, and he knew she would soon express it.

She leaned forward. "I'm sorry. I know this isn't what you expected. It's not the way we should be."

The coffee boiled, and he pulled it from the fire and poured her a cup. "Tell me—how should we be?"

He handed her the cup, taking in the way her hair caught the fire's light, the way her skin glowed. He didn't need to see the darkening of her cheeks to sense her discomfort at the way he stared.

She angled toward the fire. "You know—man and wife."

He grimaced at the way she gulped the hot liquid. He turned his own cup round and round, letting the silence force her to explain herself.

"You said the very first day you didn't expect romance but wanted a real marriage."

"Yup." It wasn't exactly how he had put it but close enough.

"I know what that means," she whispered.

"Good." He downed several swallows

"It's just that with the children and all—" Her voice trailed off.

He studied the flames without answering.

"You"—she gulped—"you aren't wishing they weren't with us, are you?"

"Me?" He jerked to his feet. "Ain't I been good to them? Can't you tell I care about them?"

"Yes."

"Well, then?" What more could he do? What did she want?

She shrugged, a helpless little gesture that made him want to kick himself for his outburst.

"Sometimes I think—I wonder—" She took a gusty breath. "It's so different from what I imagine you expected."

He chuckled. "Are you gonna tell me it's what you expected?"

She shot him a startled look, then slowly grinned. "Not in my wildest dreams," she admitted.

Her mischievous look did wild things to his pulse rate, but he corralled his thoughts and held her gaze. "So what do we do except take each day as it comes?"

He heard her swallow. She blinked and opened her mouth twice before she got the words past her lips. "Nothing, I suppose."

But he heard the doubtful tone in her voice and searched his mind for some way of letting her know he was willing to wait for the right time—and some indication from her as to when she was ready. But before he could find the words, he heard a rumble.

"Someone's comin'." He stood and reached for his rifle.

She edged over to stand close to him.

"Hello, the camp!" a man's voice called as a wagon drew near. A man and woman sat on the seat. "Any objections to us joining you's all?"

"It's as much your right as mine," Crane replied, studying the pair—a middle-aged couple with a weathered leanness that made him uneasy.

"We was looking for a nice place to stop and saw your fire," the lady drawled.

The man took in the sleeping children and nodded to the

other side of the clearing. "We'll park over there." He swung the wagon around.

Three youngsters sat on the end gate, two good-sized boys and a half-grown girl.

Crane glanced toward Ted and Betsy. Although Ted lay motionless, his eyes were open. Crane sank to the ground next to the children, and Ted whispered, "I don't like them."

"No reason not to," Crane whispered. "They're heading west same as us. And they're minding their own business." In fact, since they'd entered the camp, they'd turned their backs and kept their distance.

He waited until the other family settled down, then slipped into the darkness to check on the horses, leading them closer for the night. He moved the packs next to the bedroll.

"Crane?" Maggie whispered.

"Just being cautious," he muttered.

He slept with one eye open and his rifle at his side and woke at dawn. A quick glance assured him their neighbors were still asleep, and nothing had been disturbed. *Gettin' jumpy,* he scolded himself, rising to build a small fire and put the coffee to boil.

Maggie uncurled from her bed and joined him. "Should we call out to them?" she asked.

He shook his head. " 'Spect they'll get up when they got a mind."

"I don't mind telling you I'm anxious to get moving." She rubbed the back of her neck.

Crane straightened and studied her. "You sleep all right?"

She grimaced. "I must have slept crooked. My neck is hurting."

"Let me rub it." He placed his hands on her taut shoulders, his thumbs on her neck. He knew the moment he touched her he'd made a mistake. Fire flared up his limbs and grabbed his throat so he couldn't breathe. His arms felt like wooden posts. He rubbed firm circles along her shoulder muscles and up her neck.

"Good morning, y'all."

At the sound of the other man's voice, Crane dropped his hands, pressing his palms to his hips. " 'Morning." He stepped toward the man, extending his hand. "Name's Crane. This here's my wife." He nodded his head toward Maggie, then indicated the children. "These are our young'uns, Ted and Betsy."

Ted kept his stare on the strangers, while Betsy, bleary eyed and half awake, struggled to a sitting position.

"Hiram Johns." The man shook his hand. "Wife, Jean, and my youngsters. That there is Billy." He indicated the bigger boy who was rolling up his blanket. "That's Joe." The other boy was almost as tall and a bit on the pudgy side. "The gal is Annie." The girl was still curled up on her blanket. "She ain't been feeling too well."

"Coffee?" Crane held out the pot.

"Don't mind if I do. Say, but ain't it been a hot one?" The man settled down to visit, while his boys ran into the bush for more wood and the missus gathered up food for their breakfast.

Crane scowled at the man, wondering why he wasn't helping with the camp chores, but the man talked on about weather and horses and trains and too many things for Crane to keep track of. He helped Maggie prepare oatmeal porridge, and while they ate, Hiram Johns talked nonstop.

Finally Crane interrupted. "Guess we best get packed up." He tromped toward the horses. "Talks more'n an old woman," he muttered under his breath as he fixed the pack on the horse.

Usually Ted helped with getting the horses ready, but this morning he had run off with the other youngsters to explore the grove of trees. Crane had no mind to rob him of a few minutes of play.

A noise skittered through the air. Crane stopped and listened. It sounded like Betsy. Then he heard it again, small and thin, like Betsy in a panic.

He dropped the saddle and headed toward the sound, sliding soundlessly between the trees. The children were ahead of him. Billy, the older boy, had Betsy by one arm. She grunted, trying to free herself. Crane's jaw tightened at the way Billy's hand squeezed her thin arm.

Billy threw something.

"Stop that." Betsy squealed and tried again to pull away.

Then Crane saw why Betsy was so upset. Cat was up the tree, hissing as Billy threw stones at her.

"You leave my cat alone," Betsy demanded again, tears running down her face as Billy squeezed harder. "Let go of me. You're hurting."

Billy laughed, a sound that made Crane grit his teeth. "What's the matter? Does the little baby think I'm gonna hurt her poor little kitty?"

The other boy chanted. "Poor kitty. Poor kitty. Hit him again, Billy."

And the half-grown girl muttered, "Aw, who cares about a cat? Let's go get somethin' to eat."

"In a minute," Billy growled, raising his arm again.

Crane was about to break into the clearing when Ted ambled over to the bigger boy. Calm and quiet, he stepped to Billy's side and clenched the boy's wrist. "Think you better go now. And you can let Betsy go now too."

Billy pushed his face close to Ted. "You gonna make me?"

Ted glared into his face. "If I have to."

The other two gathered close. "Fight. Fight," Joe chanted.

Ted did not back down. "Let her go."

Crane took two steps and dropped his hand on Billy's shoulder. "Best do as he says."

Billy jerked away as if Betsy's arm had scalded him, and all three children spun around to face him, their eyes wide with fright.

"Best go on back to your folks."

His eyes wide, Billy dashed after his brother and sister.

"Betsy, get Cat and go stay with Maggie." His gaze lingered on Ted as Betsy ran to the tree to call Cat. "I'm proud of you, Son."

A shudder crossed Ted's shoulders. "Now let's get those horses ready and get outta here."

Crane and Ted quickly got the horses ready and led them to camp. "Let's get moving." He waited for Maggie to mount, then lifted Betsy up.

"I want to ride with Ted."

"Not today."

"Aww." She prepared to protest, but Maggie interrupted.

"Not today, Betsy." There was a hard note in her voice.

Crane quirked an eyebrow at her.

"Betsy told me what happened," she muttered. "Let's get out of here."

"I'm with you." He was about to kick Rebel's sides when the sound of metal on metal made the hair on the back of his neck stand up.

eight

Crane lifted his hands several inches into the air and slowly turned to face the Johnses. A pistol glared from the man's grubby fist. Crane sensed a meanness that accompanied cowardice. "What's this I hear 'bout you giving my boys a hard time?" If Crane had been alone, he would bluff his way out, but with Maggie and the children—he swallowed hard. "What is it you're wanting, Johns?"

The man's look darted to Maggie, a few feet away.

Crane's hands squeezed into fists as rage flooded through him. He wanted to trample the man under Rebel's hooves.

Maggie shot Crane a hard look. He knew she knew. She held his gaze, tipping her head so slightly he knew no one would have noticed but him. Instantly he understood her intent, and he twitched in his saddle. *No, don't do it!* But he couldn't scream the words at her.

He widened his eyes, signaling he understood, and almost choked when her lips twitched.

Her hands tightened on the reins. She yelled and kicked Liberty's sides. The horse lunged forward, right into Johns, who threw his arms up to shield himself. Crane jerked the gun from the man's hand.

Maggie reined in, glowering down at Johns. "You're lucky I don't let my horse tromp all over you."

Crane hid a grin. Maggie would have taken great delight in doing so. He tucked the gun into his waistband and turned to face the man.

"Next time you feel like gettin' all hot and bothered about them sons of yers, you best make sure to get the story right." He nodded for Maggie and Ted to ride. "I'll be leaving yer gun out there." He nodded toward the road. "You can go and get it when it suits ya."

He reined around and paused. "Y'all have a nice day now," he said and trotted after the others.

As they rode away, the humor of the situation hit him, and he roared with laughter.

Maggie crunched her brows together. "What's so funny?"

"You. You're somethin' else." He couldn't stop grinning at her, enjoying the way her eyes widened at his words.

"What do you mean?" Her tone held a note of belligerence.

"Ain't you scared of nothin'?"

Her forehead furrowed. "I vowed I'd never turn away from nothing."

He chuckled. "Well, so far, I'd say you got a pretty good record."

Her eyes rounded. "You laughing at me?"

His grin widened. "Could be." He scratched his neck. "Or could be I'm just tickled."

Her gaze held a challenge. He knew his grin was as wide as the open prairie, but he couldn't seem to help it. And for the life of him he couldn't say whether it was amusement or admiration that had him staring at her like a moonstruck cowpoke.

"Crane," Betsy sobbed. "I'm scared." Her eyes pooled with tears, then overflowed in a glistening trail down each cheek. Her distress was like the sting of a whip.

"They ain't going to hurt you. Isn't that right, Ted?"

"You bet," the boy grunted.

Crane saw a reflection of his own concern in Maggie's eyes. Betsy had more than her fair share of scares in the past day or so. She'd do with some careful watching. On the other hand—he slanted a look at Ted—the boy was proving he had plenty of guts.

"They'll never catch us," he assured Betsy. "Not in that old wagon of theirs and with that old moth-eaten bag of bones pulling it."

Betsy giggled at his description of the horse.

"Why, I've seen better horses put out to pasture." Crane

increased their pace a fraction. It was true—the Johnses didn't have a hope in the world of catching them, but he wasn't a man to test his luck.

"She puts me in mind of an old horse we got in a trade one time when we picked up a bunch for Mr. Burrows. I don't know how they slipped her in." He chuckled. "Turns out it was the same old crock Burrows had included in a trade three years earlier. I think she made the trip around a number of traders before someone finally took pity on her."

He amused them with more stories of his cowboy days until the sun hung high overhead. "There's another water tower."

They filled their canteens and watered the horses; then, remembering the roaring train of yesterday, they rode a distance from the tracks before taking a noon break.

After another cold lunch, Ted stood. "Think I'll take a walk."

"Where's Ted going?" Betsy asked, jumping to her feet as Ted and Cat sauntered away.

"He's stretching his legs for a bit."

Crane studied the child more closely. She rocked back and forth on her feet, twisting a corner of her skirt, her face screwed up with worry.

"We can see him real well." He waved his arms. "You could walk for a week without getting lost."

But she didn't relax.

Maggie eased to his side and leaned close, grabbing his arm to pull herself up to whisper in his ear. "She's been tense and restless all morning."

He broke into a cold sweat at her touch, and for a split second, he forgot his concern for the child. Then with iron self-control, he pushed aside his reaction to Maggie to focus on Betsy. "I don't know what we should do about her."

He held to his self-control by a thread as he breathed in Maggie's scent—rich with the smell of sage and fresh grass. A strand of hair wafted across his cheek. He closed his eyes and sucked in heated air.

"I don't see what we can do except let her know we'll

take care of her."

He knew the minute she stepped away. It made it possible for him to breathe again.

Betsy remained fretful all afternoon, crying when they rode too fast, moaning that she was tired, and screaming in alarm when a rabbit bounced across the trail.

More than once Maggie gave Crane a worried look. He shrugged. He was worried about Betsy too, but he didn't have a notion what to do about it.

Several times Crane caught a glimpse of a dark fringe off to the right. "You keep to the trail," he told Maggie. "I'm going to see if there's a creek over there." After ten minutes' riding, he suddenly overlooked a narrow, green valley with a band of dark water winding through it and trees crowding down the banks.

He pushed his hat back. "I'll be a skinned snake. If that ain't the nicest thing I've seen in many a day." He pushed his hat down firm on his head and raced back to the others.

"There's a good spot for camp over here," he called. It was early to stop, but maybe Betsy was plumb tired. She fussed as they set up camp and prepared a meal.

"You want to help cook some biscuits?" Crane asked her.

"No. Where's Maggie?"

"She's gone to get water."

It was the first time Betsy hadn't hung over his shoulder drooling as she waited for the food to cook.

When Maggie returned, Betsy grabbed her hand, pulling her close to Crane so she could hold his hand too. "Ted, where are you?" she called. And when he answered, she insisted he sit in front of her.

"I have to get up to get the food." Maggie laughed, and Betsy reluctantly let her go. But as soon as they each had a plate, the child again insisted Maggie sit close. She only let go of Crane's hand to allow him to eat. His concern deepened considerably when she picked at her food.

Maggie noticed too. "Betsy, aren't you hungry?"

"Not much." The child pushed her plate away. "I keep thinking I hear those people coming after us."

"Oh, Sweetie." Maggie set her plate down and pulled Betsy to her lap. "You remember what I told you about God?"

Betsy pressed into her embrace. "What?"

"He'll always take care of us. Remember?"

The child tipped her head so she could see Maggie's face. "Was He taking care of us back there?"

Maggie stroked the tangled blond locks. "Well, we was scared, but nothing bad really happened. So I guess He was."

Crane considered her answer. Maybe he'd been thinking the same thing as Betsy, doubting as much as she, but what Maggie said made sense.

Betsy thought hard for a moment. "I was so scared. Especially when that bad man had a gun."

Crane laughed. "I don't think you need to worry, Betsy. Maggie will always come to our rescue." He sobered. "I'll never let anything happen to you either if I can help it."

"Me neither," Ted murmured.

A pleased look on her face, Betsy cuddled against Maggie. "I'm not so scared now."

Crane mussed her hair. "Good, 'cause it's hard to do anything with you holding on to us all."

She giggled a little and let Maggie set her aside to clean up.

That night, the four of them lay side by side. Maggie had read until Betsy fell asleep.

Ted's voice came out of the darkness. "Where was God when Pa sold me to that man?"

Crane tensed. How would Maggie explain this?

At first she didn't answer. Then she sighed deeply. "I don't know why bad things happen. I just know they do. Ma used to say it was because everybody can choose whether to do right or wrong, and when someone chooses wrong, then it starts a whole chain of events. And sometimes innocent people get hurt."

"You mean 'cause Pa did something wrong, I had to pay

for it?" Ted's voice rose.

Crane felt the same incredulous disbelief. Why should Ted or, for that matter, Betsy, pay for something they had no part in?

"Guess maybe whatever we do affects somebody else." Maggie's voice grew stronger. "But we needn't use it as an excuse." She wasn't making any sense.

"What do you mean?" Crane asked.

"Sometimes people say they're mean because someone was unfair to them. Or they say, 'if you had to live like I did, you wouldn't be so nice either.' I don't think one has to lead to the other. Do you know what I mean?"

He grunted. "I guess."

"And don't you think God played a part when we 'happened' to ride down the road that 'happened' to go past the farm where Ted was and that we 'happened' to stop there to buy some food? Ted, what are the chances, do you suppose?"

"Not very good," the boy mumbled.

"Not a chance in the world we would have found you except for one thing." She paused for effect. "God. God led us there."

Crane let the thought settle into his mind. She had a point. Fact was she had made several of them that somehow managed to upset the way he figured things. He looked at the sky. The stars were so close he felt he could reach out and grab a handful. Somehow God seemed just as close and real. The idea of God being close enough to touch made him feel warm and good inside.

Before it was light, he wakened to a strange sound. Immediately he recognized it was Betsy moaning in her sleep. She flung her arms out and moaned again. She must be dreaming.

He reached over and shook her. "Betsy, wake up." He jerked his hand back and sat bolt upright.

"Maggie." He reached over both children to shake her shoulder. "Maggie, wake up." But she shrugged. "Maggie," he insisted, shaking harder. "Come on—wake up."

She opened one eye slowly. "It's still nighttime." She pulled the covers to her chin.

"Maggie," he growled, trying to keep his voice down so he wouldn't disturb Ted. He shook her hard, like a dog shaking an old boot.

"What's the matter with you?" she groaned. "Can't you let a body sleep?"

"Not now. I think Betsy's sick."

Covering her eyes with her arm, she groaned. He watched her fight her way to consciousness. Slowly she sat up, leaning over her knees, her head lolling almost on her chest. "What did you say?" she finally managed.

"It's Betsy. I think she's sick."

"Oh."

He shook his head. It was a long ways from her ears to her brain. "Come on, Maggie. Wake up."

"I'm awake," she mumbled. "See—my eyes are open."

He waved a hand in front of her face. "Hello? Anybody home?"

"Very funny," she muttered. "Don't suppose coffee's ready."

"Not yet. I just woke up. Betsy was moaning. I thought she was dreaming, but she's hot."

"Well, why didn't you say so?" She shot him a cross look as she pushed the blanket back and struggled to her feet, mumbling, "Life would be a lot simpler if people would just say what they wanted."

"What's the matter?" Ted sat up.

"I think Betsy's sick," Crane said. "Could you get up and get the fire going for coffee? I think your sister could use some."

Maggie bent over Betsy and felt her forehead. "She's fevered all right. Here, Sweetie—let me check you over."

In the flare of Ted's fire, Maggie checked Betsy's back and tummy, then looked over her legs. "I don't see any rash." She straightened. "I don't know what's wrong with her, but we won't be traveling today."

Of course they couldn't travel with a sick child. "How long

do you suppose she'll be sick?"

She shrugged. "Your guess is as good as mine. That coffee ready yet, Ted?"

Crane took the cup of coffee Ted offered and sat deep in thought. Laying over gave the Johnses a chance to catch up. Then there was the problem of food. He had hoped to purchase some more supplies soon. He eyed the creek. A good place for game. He'd go hunting instead.

"I'm going to check on things," he announced and climbed the steep bank, lying on his stomach to watch the trail. He had a good clear view of the trail for miles. He turned toward the camp. It was down far enough that he was certain it would be invisible from the trail. "I'll just have to keep a careful watch," he muttered.

Returning to the camp, he found Maggie giving Betsy some water. "Food's ready," she murmured, nodding toward the fire.

He helped himself and, when he finished, said, "I'm going hunting." He turned to Ted. "I want you to climb that draw." He pointed toward the narrow vee leading to the crest of the bank. "Keep down but look sharp to the trail. Let Maggie know if anybody heads this way." He dug the pistol from his saddlebag and handed it to Maggie. "I need the rifle, but I'll leave this with you."

"We'll be fine."

Betsy slept, her cheeks flushed, her arms flung out.

"You sure?" He didn't mean only the risk of strangers.

Maggie gave him a direct look. "Sleep is probably the best thing for her." She waved a hand. "You go on now."

He hesitated, torn between the desire to guard them and the need for food; then nodding, he headed into the slight breeze. He saw evidence of abundant game but knew there would be none within sound of camp, so he kept a brisk pace along the bare banks of the creek for a spell, then eased into the trees, moving more slowly and quietly. He saw several does with fawns at their sides, but it was some time before he spotted a young buck and brought it down with one shot. He dressed it out, taking as much meat as he thought they could use before it spoiled. Heaving the gunnysack of meat over his shoulder, he headed back.

When he could see the camp in the distance, he scoured the banks and caught a patch of dark indicating Ted's position. *Good boy.*

As he drew closer, he looked for Maggie. She lay close to Betsy, both sleeping. Her eyelashes drew dark half moons on her cheeks. The heat painted dull pink in her face, and her dark hair flung out like a glistening black spray. His steps faltered. She was so beautiful.

The child shifted, and Maggie sat up to check on Betsy. She saw Crane and smiled.

At the look of welcome in her eyes, his ribs clamped tight.

"You did all right." She lifted a finger to indicate the sack over his shoulder.

"Yup." He shrugged from under his burden. "How's Betsy?"

"Sleeping lots."

"That good or bad?"

"Seems good to me."

He washed the meat in the slow-moving water of the creek. Then, ignoring the heat, he built an efficient little fire and set several hunks of meat to roast.

"Broth would be good for Betsy," Maggie said, so he put a slab to boil.

Then he straightened. "I better relieve Ted." He climbed the hill to the boy. "See anything of note?"

Ted shrugged. "A couple of riders headed west. They didn't even look this way."

"Fine. You did a good job, Son. Now go down and keep your sister company while I sit guard."

The day passed slowly. Ted brought him food at noon, but still Crane kept watch. Once or twice he thought it might all be for nothing, but he couldn't relax until he had seen the Johnses pass.

It was late afternoon before he heard the creaking wagon.

They came into sight. Even without the noise he would have known them. As he'd told Betsy, the horse was a sorry sight. So was the wagon—the canvas torn and flapping on one side. They ambled past without a sideways look and rattled on west.

Crane nodded. He watched the trail a bit longer. "That's that," he mumbled. Not to say there weren't other people they should be wary of, but he calculated the Johnses were the biggest threat they were likely to encounter for a few days, and he rejoined the others.

Betsy woke off and on during the evening and slept fitfully during the night. Crane got up several times to get her a drink or talk softly to settle her.

The next morning she sat up and said, "My froat hurts." Her hoarse voice was proof of her distress.

Maggie fixed warm tea and fed her several spoonfuls before the child lay down and slept.

Worry made Crane's insides stiff. He knew nothing about children and their illnesses.

Maggie met his searching look, and her expression softened. "Don't look so worried. I think she's some better."

"But her throat?"

"I know. But her fever is gone."

He looked at the sleeping child. It was true; her cheeks had lost the flush of yesterday. "Sure hope she's better soon."

Maggie shrugged. "We'll just have to wait until she is."

The enforced idleness proved difficult to bear. Ted and Crane took turns climbing the hill. Ted took Cat for a walk along the creek.

"I'll sit with Betsy awhile if you want to go too," Crane offered.

Maggie's eyes lit. "I'd love to." She gave Betsy a long look. The child slept quietly.

"Thanks, Crane." She flashed him a wide smile.

Long after she was out of sight, Crane clung to the thought of that smile, so warm and— It felt as if she'd reserved that smile just for him. He'd been waiting for a sign from her that she was ready for more in their relationship. Was this it? He rubbed the back of his neck. Or was he grasping at straws tossed in the wind?

He had supper cooking when Maggie and Ted reappeared.

"Sorry to be gone so long," Maggie called. "We got to talking."

Betsy wakened and took more broth, then drifted back to sleep.

"Ted and I were talking about what it was like when Pa turned to the bottle."

Her blue eyes blazing at him made Crane's heart pound as if he'd run a footrace.

"I think about all Ted remembers is how afraid he was. Ma was gone. Pa was suddenly mean and unpredictable. And then I was gone for days at a time." Her voice thickened. "I tried to spare Ted, but it was impossible." She paused. "I will never understand why Pa suddenly turned against us."

Crane knew much of this and wondered why Maggie was bringing it up again.

Her eyes flashed. "I was thinking about how it must have been for you. How you must have felt." She stopped, and in the waiting silence, Crane knew she was expecting an answer.

"I don't remember much. It was so long ago," he murmured.

She blinked. "But you said your ma died this past winter."

He clenched his hands. How was he to explain? "Doesn't seem she was there all that much, then I was away working most of the time."

Her look insisted on more.

"I can't rightly remember a time when I had either parent."

"How did you feel?"

He turned to stare at the fire. "Like I said, it was a long time ago."

"I know." She paused. "But I think some things never let us go. For instance, will I ever really trust someone again after what Pa did? There's a little bit of me that says to watch out when things look good. There might be a sudden stop to it all.

"And Ted. Will he always jerk back when someone raises their hand? Do you suppose that years from now, if someone hurts him someway, he might withdraw into himself like he was when we found him?"

Crane didn't answer. How could he?

"What about you?" Her voice dropped to a whisper.

"What about me?"

She gulped before she answered. "Do you fear getting close to people, thinking if you do, they'll disappoint you, maybe even leave you?"

His fists balled into tight knots. "You crazy? Here I am with a wife and two children, and you say I avoid getting close." He pointed at the bedrolls side by side. "How much closer can you get than that?"

"I didn't mean to upset you," she murmured, her face filled with distress. "But that's not the kind of closeness I mean."

Her words stung. He had shared more of himself with Maggie than anyone before in his life, and here she stood accusing him of avoiding closeness. He shoved more wood on the fire. "I haven't the foggiest notion what you're talking about." Then he stalked to the creek bank.

How could he have hit so far from the mark? Here he was thinking Maggie was as attracted to him as he was to her, that any day now she would indicate she wanted more from their relationship; instead she dealt him a vicious blow to the gut. Where on earth did she get her crazy ideas?

"Crane?" Her worried voice stopped him in his tracks.

"What?" He barely managed to keep the annoyance from his voice.

"Are you really mad at me?"

He could hear the fear in her voice. It drove the anger from him. "I guess not."

"I'm sorry. I don't know what I was doing. Guess maybe talking to Ted started a bunch of fears and worries in my mind." She gulped, and her voice fell to a whisper. "Sometimes it's like I say, I think this is too good and something will happen to ruin it."

"What's too good?"

"Us. You and me and the children. Heading to a new home. All that."

"And what do you suppose could ruin it?"

"You could get fed up and leave."

It was the same old thing—Maggie wanting promises for happy ever after, a promise he couldn't make 'cause he had no way of being sure he could keep it.

"Maggie, I don't know what you want me to say or do. I've been a loner most of my life." He knew she would interpret that as proof he feared closeness, so he hurried on to explain. "Didn't have much choice. Cowboys drift from job to job. It don't give them much chance to make long-lasting friendships. My point is, this is the closest I've been to anybody since"—if he said, since he was a kid, she'd take that wrong too—"since I left home to work. My point is, I'm doing the best I can." It stung to think it wasn't good enough for her.

"Crane." She grabbed his forearms. She was so close he could feel her warm breath. "I am very, very sorry." Her arms stole around his waist, and she buried her head against his chest.

With a muffled groan, he wrapped his arms around her, his face in her hair.

"Please don't think I was complaining about anything you do. I guess I really don't know what I was trying to say." She paused. "Promise you won't leave us."

"Oh, Maggie," he groaned, barely able to sort out his thoughts. "I don't intend to leave. Why would I? This is the best I've ever known of life."

He could feel her nodding.

They stood hugging each other, offering comfort in the most basic of ways. But Crane knew a stirring deep within. A longing for more. The urgency of the feeling, the yawning depth of the emotion it exposed, sent a shudder up his spine.

"Maybe we should get back to camp."

Later, after they had all settled down for the night, Crane lay awake a long time. His anger had long ago disappeared; yet his mind went round and round with questions. Did he shy away from closeness as Maggie suggested? Or had she been goading him to make promises of security and happiness?

Why had he pulled away when there was every reason to think Maggie might have welcomed a kiss. . .and maybe even more?

What had she said about some things never letting us go? For the first time in years, he purposely turned his thoughts back to the time his pa left. How had he felt? But it was as he told Maggie; he could barely remember. He did remember how it left him feeling so exposed he'd promised himself he'd never let himself be open to that feeling again.

He folded his arms behind his head. Maybe Maggie was right. He cared about these people, but inside was a part of him he guarded. Put it down to experience, even maturity—a person had to keep back some portion of himself or face the threat of being destroyed.

Something tickled his nose, pulling him from his sleep, and he brushed it aside. A giggle close to his ear snapped his eyes open.

"Hi." Betsy giggled again. "It's morning."

"You must be feeling better."

"I'm hungry."

He snorted. "You're better." His arms snaked out and grabbed the little girl, pressing her to his chest. "And I'm glad."

She giggled and squirmed out of his arms, jumping to her feet. "Come on. It's time to get up."

He laughed as he jumped up. "And time to get breakfast?" he teased.

"Uh-huh."

There was a festive feeling as they broke camp and returned to the trail.

nine

They stopped early in the afternoon at a grove of trees set back from the road. Crane unsaddled the horses while Maggie and the children gathered wood.

Later, he and Maggie lingered over coffee while Ted and Betsy chased Cat through the trees.

"They both seem to be happy now, don't they?"

"Yeah, I reckon." He listened to their laughter and the rustling of the leaves. Didn't seem to take much to make them happy—full tummies and safety. "What about you, Maggie?"

"Me, what?"

"Are you happy? What does it take to make you happy?" He'd been aching to know. It festered that he seemed to have fallen short.

She stared at the fire a long time. He could tell by the way she pressed her finger to her bottom lip that she was thinking. "After Ma died, I didn't know if I could be happy again. I learnt to take care of myself. I could find a way to earn enough money to buy my food, and I made it clear I didn't put up with no nonsense. I was careful too. But you know—"

She was sitting a few feet from him, but now she turned and leaned toward him, almost touching his knees, her face turned up at him. The light danced in her hair and slanted across her face, and he caught his breath at her beauty. All he had to do was lift his hand and cup her chin. But he kept perfectly still, wanting something more from her, though he couldn't say what.

She continued. "It wasn't enough."

It was as if his body acted of its own accord as he leaned forward, resting his elbows on his knees so their noses were

116

but a few inches apart. Their gazes bridged the distance until he felt her intense stare reach down into his soul and stir a cauldron of emotions.

She swallowed hard and moistened her lips. "I guess part of it was I'd forgotten about God. But I think there was more to it. I found what I want right here."

His lungs felt like wood. His heart thundered in his ears. A silent cry called from deep inside. He didn't know what it was he wanted or how to still the cry; all he could do was wait for her to explain herself.

"It's this." She circled her hand to indicate the camp. "It's you and the children." Her gaze returned to him. "The people I care about."

His throat constricted for a heartbeat, then a warm feeling flooded upward. For the first time since last night he could fill his lungs without his breath catching.

"How about you, Crane?"

"Huh?" Her question pulled him from his jumbled thoughts.

"What does it take to make you happy?"

"I'm easy to satisfy. My needs are simple, my wants few."

Happy wasn't something he'd given much thought to in the past. About the only dream he'd ever had was to move west when he was free to go.

಄

Several days later, the sun was high in the brazen sky, pouring its fury upon their heads, when Ted, riding at Crane's side, mumbled, "Wagon ahead."

"I see." He'd seen it for a mile or so. "Slow down a bit. We'll take our time about catching up."

It was possible they had caught up to the Johnses, but he heard no ominous screech, and two horses seemed to be pulling the wagon. Besides, it rode with a certain grace the Johnses' wagon lacked.

Slowly they closed the distance until Crane could see two young boys perched on the tailgate. One turned to call something over his shoulder, and a man's head appeared around the side of the wagon. He waved a greeting.

Crane could now see the two boys well enough to make out that they were as alike as peas in a pod, the same sandy hair, the same blue eyes. He was sure every freckle matched.

"Twins." Maggie edged her horse closer to his side.

"Yup." He couldn't remember seeing twins before and forced his gaze away so he wouldn't be guilty of staring.

A quick glance to either side and he knew Betsy and Ted were as tense as broncs in a corral. He pushed his hat back and scratched his head. "You hold back while I ride on ahead." He slapped the reins and trotted up beside the driver. It was a young man and, at his side, a young woman with a babe in her arms. "Howdy," he called.

The man pulled the wagon to a halt. "Howdy. Saw you coming up behind us." He held out a hand. "Wally Strong. Pleased to meet you."

Crane shook hands as he made a quick assessment of the pair. They had frank, open expressions, friendly eyes, and wide smiles. He decided he liked them.

"My wife, Sally Jane." The man put an arm around his wife, pulling her close.

Crane motioned the others forward and introduced them.

Matching faces poked out on either side of the parents, and Sally Jane laughed. "My boys, Matt"—she nodded to the one on her right—"And Mark"—she smiled at the one on her left.

Crane wondered how she could tell one from the other.

The infant squirmed, and Sally Jane sat her up. "And our daughter, Sarah."

The little one's eyes widened at the sight of so many strangers; then she saw Betsy and gurgled, reaching out her arms.

Betsy beamed. "She's so sweet."

"We were thinking about taking a noon break," Wally said. "Perhaps you folks would like to join us."

Crane felt everyone's gaze turn to him and nodded. "Why not?"

Over their meal Crane asked, "Where you headed?"

Wally looked thoughtful. "I've been looking for land that's good for farming." His gaze swept the horizon. "This appeals—no trees, level."

Crane nodded. "We're thinking to go as far as Calgary before we look for something."

As he talked, he watched Maggie holding the baby and talking to her. It looked so natural. Then Maggie lifted her head and met his eyes. A deep yearning stirred in the pit of his stomach. It looked so right to see Maggie with an infant. *If only it was mine.*

He swallowed hard. Where had that come from? He was grateful when Wally's voice drew him back to reality.

"We'll be settling before that. As soon as we find land close to the rail line."

"Wally," Sarah Jane called softly. "Ask them to ride with us for a spell."

He smiled at her across the clearing. "The very thing I was thinking." He held her gaze a moment more before he turned to Crane. "How about it?"

Crane saw the eager flash in Maggie's eyes. Perhaps it was just the thing they needed to erase the remnants of fear left by their encounter with the Johnses. "Sounds good." He was rewarded by a warm smile from Maggie.

They hadn't gone far when one of the twins crawled to his father's side. "Pa, can we get down and walk?"

"Us too, Crane?" Betsy asked.

Wally reined in the wagon. "It's fine with me, if Crane approves."

"I don't know." Crane stared down the trail, pretending reluctance. "You might not be able to keep up. Or"—he rubbed his chin—"you might get lost."

"Aww," Betsy slumped.

"He's joshing us," Ted muttered, but the worried look didn't leave his face until Crane grinned and nodded.

Whooping, Ted jumped down, and Crane tied Ted's horse

to the back of the wagon.

Ted raced down the road, shouting over his shoulder, "Can't catch me!"

The twins barreled off the wagon and tore after him.

"Hurry, Maggie," Betsy begged as Maggie reached around to hand her down. The child barely waited for her feet to touch the ground before she lit after them, calling, "Wait for me!" Cat raced after her.

Wally chuckled. "Could be we'll be the ones having to hustle to keep up." And he clucked at the horses. Maggie rode at Sally Jane's side. Sally Jane turned to her. "I can't help but notice the children call you by your first names. It seems a little unusual."

"They aren't our children," Maggie hastened to explain. "At least not in the usual way. Ted's my brother, and Betsy—"

"Betsy was a waif we found on our travels," Crane supplied.

"First day we were married." Maggie chuckled.

Crane pressed his lips together. He wished she hadn't said that. It was like begging for more questions. And he was right.

"Really." Sally Jane perked up. "How long have you been married then?"

"Almost a month." Maggie's tone said she regretted having opened the door to their curiosity.

Silence followed Maggie's answer. Crane stared straight ahead. He could almost hear their questions.

Sally Jane nodded. "Newlyweds then. Congratulations to you both."

Maggie murmured her thanks.

"A waif? Such a beautiful child." The young woman shifted so she could see Maggie better. "Tell me how you found her."

"Now, Sally Jane, it's none of our business," Wally warned.

"You're absolutely right. Forgive me, Maggie." She dipped her head to Crane. "You too, Crane."

" 'S'all right," he murmured, feeling tight inside at her embarrassment. Suddenly he hooted with laughter. "But truth is—it's too good a story to keep to ourselves."

"Crane," Maggie muttered. Her cheeks stained dull red.

"You should have seen her square off against—" He searched for some way to describe Bull without being indecent. He finally said it the best way he could find. "Betsy has no parents, and this man thought he owned her."

Wally shot him a shocked look.

"Anyway, didn't matter to Maggie that he was bigger and meaner. She marched up to him bold as could be and ordered him to drop the child."

Sally Jane stared at him. "And did he?"

"He took some persuading." Crane chuckled.

"I threatened to shoot him," Maggie muttered.

Crane's smile deepened. Despite Maggie's uncomfortable squirming, he was afraid he'd pop the buttons on his shirt.

Then Wally chuckled too. "Bet she led you a merry chase before you caught her."

Crane's mouth tightened. He wondered what they would say if he told them he met her, married her, and rode out with Betsy all in the space of a few hours.

"Don't remember her putting up much of a fight," he mumbled and, glancing out of the corner of his eyes, saw the tips of Maggie's ears turn bright red.

They overtook the children at that point.

"Cat keeps yowling to be carried!" Ted called.

Wally slowed the wagon. "Put her in the back."

Ted set the cat inside, and the children dropped behind, skipping along in the dust.

They rode together the rest of the day, and by mutual consent pulled into a treed area for the night.

"Boys, gather up some firewood," Wally told the twins.

"Come on, Ted," one of them called, and the boys scampered away.

Betsy hung close to Sally Jane. "Can I hold the baby?"

"Of course you can." Sally Jane patted the ground beside her. "You sit right here, and you can hold her as long as you like."

The baby stared at Betsy, then cooed. Crane had heard others speak about heartstrings being tugged, but this was the first time he'd felt it.

He turned to Wally. "Let's go find some fresh meat."

"Do you need anything before I go?" Wally addressed his wife.

Sally Jane waved a hand, her focus on the baby. "You go ahead."

They found partridges and a couple of rabbits. As they returned, the smell of wood smoke and coffee greeted them. Maggie and Sally Jane looked up as the men approached.

Crane watched the eager way Sally Jane's gaze sought her husband. It brought a hollow feeling to his chest. He turned his eyes in Maggie's direction. She smiled at him. It wasn't the same intimate kind of look the other couple had exchanged, but it was warm and welcoming, and it made him want to laugh out loud.

"This is real nice, isn't it, Sally Jane?" Wally turned to Crane to explain. "She's been missing home and wishing she had someone to visit with." He chortled. "Guess she's getting tired of what I have to say."

Sally Jane laughed. "I never get tired of you, and you know it." Then she sobered. "But sometimes I think I've heard all I want about the virtues of plows and wheat and oxen." Her eyes twinkled at her husband. "It's nice to talk to someone about other things."

Crane fixed the carcasses on a spit, but his thoughts tumbled over each other. He knew he wasn't real good company on the trail, content to ride for hours without saying a word. Until now it hadn't mattered. But suddenly he wondered if Maggie wished for better company. He promised himself he'd try harder to find things she liked to talk about.

Wally turned to Maggie. "How are you enjoying the trail?"

She seemed surprised he had asked.

Crane's hands stilled as he waited for her answer.

"Just fine."

Her words sounded sincere, and Crane bent over his task, pleased he had passed muster.

"Maggie's made of pretty tough stuff," Sally Jane murmured. "She was telling me some of the things that have happened to her recently."

Crane perked up. Was their marriage one of the things that had "happened" to Maggie?

"What things?" Wally asked kindly.

Maggie swallowed hard and explained about her mother's death, her father's changed behavior, and how she'd lost track of Ted for awhile.

"Wow!" Wally rubbed his chin. "You really have been through the rocks, haven't you?" His expression gentle, he asked, "How are you doing now?"

Crane watched the expressions play across Maggie's face as she considered Wally's question. "I still miss my ma." Her voice thickened.

At the sound of her distress, Crane took a step toward her, then halted, crossing his arms over his chest.

"But my anger at Pa has gone, and it's left me able to remember all sorts of good things. We were a happy family until Ma died. I don't want to forget that. And I especially don't want Ted to forget."

"You young folk have a mighty lot on your plate," Wally murmured. "We wish you all the best." He hesitated. "And if we can help in any way, you let us know."

Maggie murmured her thanks.

Absently, Crane mumbled agreement. It was the first time he'd realized that acquiring two children carried such a heavy load, and he wondered if he'd grabbed himself a wild bronco. Then he relaxed. He'd always been the one to go for the rankest horse in the outfit 'cause he'd sooner have a horse with guts and spirit than a lead-footed nag. As he turned to check the meat, he grinned. Guess he was the same way about life. Somehow he knew he'd never have a dull moment with Maggie at his side.

After supper Sally Jane brought out a pair of scissors. "Come on, you two," she nodded at the twins. "I want to get rid of some of that hair while there's still light enough to see." She wrapped a towel around one boy and set to work cutting his sandy locks. Then she did the same to the other. Finished, she held the scissors toward Maggie. "Maybe you'd be wanting to borrow these."

Maggie's head jerked up, then she grinned at Crane. "Sounds like a good idea." She crooked her finger at him.

"Me?" He needed a haircut. Had for weeks. But it never crossed his mind he'd get it from Maggie. The idea of her hands in his hair made his mouth go dry.

"Why not? I used to cut Ted's hair all the time."

He purposely looked at Ted. The boy's hair was only getting long enough to be sure it was light brown.

"You can't blame me for that." She waited, a towel in one hand, those wretched scissors in the other. "Not afraid, are you?" she jeered.

He narrowed his eyes. "Of you or those scissors you're holding like a branding iron?" She shrugged as Wally chuckled.

Knowing he was beat, Crane pushed to his feet. He could use a good diversion right now. Say a stampede.

The fire crackled like an old woman laughing. The children squealed and laughed as they chased through the trees. But nothing came to his rescue.

Forcing his lungs to expand and his eyes to obey, he lifted his gaze upward. Fascinated, he watched a small pulse throbbing in Maggie's throat.

He tried to quiet the pounding from a surging pulse deep in his chest. Despite his determination to breath normally, his throat tightened, and he could barely suck in a gasp. His ears pounded with a deafening roar. Was it desire he saw in her eyes? Or—he forced a shaft of air into his lungs—was it simply a challenge?

He felt Wally and Sally Jane watching him and forced himself to lumber to the stool. Stiffly he sat on the smooth wood, bracing the toes of his boots in the dirt. She wrapped the towel around his shoulders. He could feel her warmth as she stood behind him. Then she ran her fingers through his hair. Fire ignited his nerves.

"Been awhile?" Her low voice fueled the fire.

His thoughts choked. *Your hair, you idiot, she's talking about your hair.* "Yup," he croaked.

"How short you want it?"

"Short." *Short enough so I never have to go through this delicious torture again.*

"Short it is."

Her hands lifted a strand of hair, and she snipped it. Other sounds faded. There was nothing but the *snip, snip, snip* of the scissors. And her nearness.

He was drowning in her nearness. Her arm brushed his shoulder. Her thigh glanced across his knee. She reached out and touched his chin with a fingertip.

"Let's see how it looks."

His lungs like steel bands, he raised his head. But he looked past her shoulder. If he met her eyes, he would lose all control.

"Not too bad so far," she murmured, her breath grazing his face, sweet as honey, warm as the summer's breeze.

Betsy skidded into the circle of light. "What'cha doing, Crane?" She leaned against his knee.

"You're gonna get hair all over you."

She grabbed a handful as she straightened, stroking it with her fingers before she pulled a lock of her own hair forward and lifted Crane's to it to compare. "Same as mine."

Betsy's was much lighter and curly, but Crane agreed. "Just about."

Satisfied, she scampered away.

Maggie stood in front of him now. "Just about done." She leaned across his knees. He felt her muscles tense and shift as she lifted her arms and took a handful of hair. She was so close. She smelled of coffee and supper and the baby she'd held. He wanted to tell her to stop. To leave the rest uncut. He wanted to beg her never to stop. He closed his eyes, wishing his ordeal was over.

By the time she finished, his muscles ached. He jerked to his feet to brush the hair off, then grabbed a cup of coffee, desperate to relieve the parched feeling in the back of his throat.

Wally stood and stretched. "Just look at that sunset!"

Flames of pink and orange and red flared across the sky.

"It's beautiful," Sally Jane murmured, going to her husband's side, leaning against him as he wrapped an arm around her shoulders.

" 'The sky is the daily bread of the eyes,' " Wally quoted. "You don't see much more sky than you do out here on the prairies."

Crane met Maggie's gaze and knew she was thinking the same as he: a bit too much sky, a bit too much nothing.

They called the children in.

"Can we sleep over there?" Matt, or was it Mark, pointed toward a clump of bushes.

"As long as you stay where we can see you." Wally handed them each a bedroll.

Crane handed Betsy her roll, but she looked up at him. "Where you going to sleep, Crane?"

"Right here." He grabbed his bundle and flipped it open a few feet from the fire.

She nodded and unrolled her bedding next to his, then stood over it, waiting for Ted to put his beside hers. "Now you, Maggie." Maggie silently obeyed.

Crane saw the glance that passed between Wally and Sally Jane, and he knew they must be wondering about the sleeping arrangements, but he didn't offer any explanation.

Maggie waited until the children were settled, then turned to the Strongs. "Crane brought his ma's Bible with him. I've been reading aloud from it every night. Do you mind?"

Sally Jane swallowed hard. "My father always read aloud at suppertime. I miss it."

Wally stared at his wife. "Why, Dear, you never told me that."

She shrugged. "Maybe it's leaving them all behind that makes me remember little things we used to do." She patted his knee. "Don't look so worried."

Silently he squeezed her hand.

Maggie waited while Crane filled his cup and got comfortable on his bedroll before she began. He didn't mean to be irreverent, but he found her voice settled through him, like sand filtering through water, until it reached its limit. A hundred things rose and flitted away before he could grab them and figure them out. Longings. Wishes. Waiting.

She closed the Bible. He hadn't heard a word.

Sally Jane sighed. "That was nice."

Ted sat up. "What does it mean?"

"It means God loves you so much He sent His only Son, whom He loved, so we—you—could live with Him forever. That's what eternal life means."

"Did He love me when I was at Dobbs's place?"

Crane had never asked, and it was the first time Ted had referred to the man by name.

Maggie wrapped her arms around him. "Of course He did." She brushed his hair back. "Did you think I had stopped loving you?"

He shook his head. "But you couldn't find me."

"That's right. Sometimes things keep people apart, but it doesn't stop their love. Same way with God. He doesn't stop loving us because somebody does something bad to us."

"You sleep now," Maggie said. She walked to the fire. Crane joined her, filling her cup, then his own.

Sally Jane sat nearby, nursing the baby. Wally took her a cup of coffee, then sat beside her.

"I can't tell you how good it's been to find you people," Sally Jane murmured.

"It's been good for us all," Maggie said. "I think Betsy and Ted have finally forgotten the Johnses."

"The Johnses?"

Maggie and Crane filled them in on their experience.

"You surely must have God's hand of protection on you," Wally said, shaking his head. "Otherwise, I don't know how you manage to get yourselves out of so many scrapes."

Maggie agreed. "I'm beginning to see that God works in many ways—big and small—when we aren't paying the least bit of attention."

Wally stretched. "Well, my dear, I think we should go to bed." He took the baby in one arm and pulled his wife to her feet, wrapping his other arm around her as he led her to the wagon.

Long after he settled down for the night, Crane heard the other couple murmuring together. *They have something special,* he thought. Something he wished he had with Maggie. He tucked his arms under his head and reminded himself he and Maggie were just beginning. They could afford to take their time. He could afford to wait for Maggie to show she was ready for more.

ten

They rode with the Strongs the next day.

"Any objection to stopping?" Wally said when they saw a line of trees.

"Nope," Crane conceded. They'd made good time all day. Besides, he wasn't in a tearing hurry.

"It's beautiful," Sally Jane said as they pushed their way through to the clearing and saw a grassy slough. "Now I can wash a few things."

The boys gathered wood, while Crane and Wally hauled water.

A little later Crane stretched out, enjoying his coffee. Maggie sat on a stool, bent over the baby, crooning. Garments of all descriptions hung on the bushes and branches. Wally or Sally Jane had gone for a walk.

He sat down beside Maggie. The baby looked at him and gurgled. When he held his hand toward her, she grabbed his index finger and pulled, chuckling.

"She likes you," Maggie said.

"She likes everybody." But he grinned, pleased at the baby's friendliness and Maggie's assessment.

"We're back," Wally called, stepping from the trees.

"How's my sweetie?" Sally Jane asked, her attention on the baby.

"Happy as a lark." Maggie reluctantly handed the infant to her mother. "She's a real sweetheart."

"I know." Sally Jane buried her nose against the baby's neck, and Wally stroked the tiny head.

"The children will be clamoring for something to eat soon," Wally said, and he and Sally Jane began preparing supper.

After the meal the children did not disappear into the trees.

Crane decided they must be tired after a long afternoon of play. Several times he thought a look passed between one of the children and Sally Jane. He couldn't rid himself of the feeling that something was up. Something he should probably know about.

He was reaching for another cup of coffee when Ted sidled up to him. "Crane," he began, "Betsy and me, we'd like to sleep with Matt and Mark tonight. Can we, please?"

Crane looked at Betsy.

"Please, Crane?" she begged.

"It's fine with me," Sally Jane said.

He studied Betsy and Ted. "You sure?"

They both nodded.

He turned to Maggie. "What do you think?"

"We'll be right here if they need us."

Crane nodded, and the children sprang to get their bedding. He turned to Maggie, muttering, "I'm betting they don't get much sleep."

She nodded.

Their beds ready, the children came back to the fire.

Wally cleared his throat. "You folks can enjoy an evening to yourselves." At the twinkle in Wally's eyes and his kindly smile, Crane's cheeks grew hot.

He heard Maggie's sharp gasp, but he dared not look at her.

"It's a surprise," Betsy said, her voice high with excitement.

Ted pulled at Crane's hands. "Come and see."

Sally Jane smiled widely. "We all worked on it."

Crane's insides felt brittle as he rose and let them lead him away from the fire.

Maggie followed, as mute as he.

They circled the slough water and turned around a large clump of bushes.

"There it is!" they called. "Just for you."

Crane stared. A pile of wood lay ready to light. A coffeepot sat on a rock. A small lean-to of willow branches squatted within comfortable distance of the fire. He narrowed his eyes.

Someone had placed their bedrolls in the tiny enclosure. His mouth turned as dry as sand as he understood their intent. He wouldn't deny he'd been longing for this day, but to be railroaded into it made him feel as awkward as a gangly newborn colt.

"Come on, children. Let's go back to our fire." Wally shepherded the children away.

Crane couldn't bring himself to look at Maggie. She cleared her throat, a grating sound screeching through his mind. "Might as well start the fire."

The fire caught and flared upward, and he stared at the flames. Ignoring the steel bands that had once been his ribs, he stepped closer. A pair of logs had been placed to sit on. He thought of sitting but couldn't seem to get the message to his legs.

The fire crackled, and a log snapped, the sound thundering along his nerves. The sharp smell of wood smoke filled his nostrils. It was all as familiar as his own name; yet tonight the scents and sounds tugged at his senses, stirring reactions totally unfamiliar. The coffee bubbled, and the smell flooded his brain.

"Coffee smells good." Was that croaking sound his voice?

She reached for the cups, and the movement drew his gaze to her. Her hair hung over her shoulders like a shiny curtain; the fire flared, sending shafts of light through the dark strands. He closed his eyes. His heart beat a tattoo inside his head.

"Coffee?"

Her voice started a riot along his nerves. He blinked and managed to take the cup she offered. Their glances touched, then danced away.

She sat on one of the logs. Coffee sloshed over the edge of his cup and stung his hand. He sucked in his breath, welcoming the pain that forced him to breathe again.

He heard her sigh softly. It was all he needed—that little sound of distress. He dropped to the other upturned log and immediately wondered if it had been wise. They were so close he could feel the warmth from her body, smell her sweetness. As he lifted his cup to drink, his elbow brushed hers. He gulped the scalding coffee.

"I had nothing to do with this," Maggie murmured, her words so low Crane could barely hear them. Or was it the pounding of his thoughts that almost drowned out her words?

"Me either."

"I suppose you can't blame them for thinking we'd be pleased."

"Yup." Was she pleased?

"After all," she hurried on, "they don't know that we've never. . ." She shrugged. "That with the children and all. . ." She trailed to a halt.

A smile tugged at the corners of Crane's mouth. Maggie, his sweet, innocent bride, always ready to state the facts boldly, was suddenly unable to speak her mind. The tension in him eased, and he leaned back. He was not one to bulldoze his way through life. The strain fled from across his shoulders. He was more than willing to let Maggie set the pace tonight. Whatever she wanted was fine with him. They had a lifetime to learn about each other and to find what pleased the other. He had no need or desire to break down gates.

"I hope the children will be all right," she said.

"They'll miss you reading to them, I expect."

"I expect." Silence settled around them, easy and comfortable.

"They sure are enjoying having some playmates," she said after a spell.

"They're a good bunch."

It had grown quite dark. To the east Crane saw a fork of lightning. "Looks like a storm building."

Maggie's head jerked up. "Where?"

Another jab of lightning was followed by distant rumbling. "It's a ways off," he said.

Flash followed flash. The thunder rolled and echoed across the plain, and the storm drew closer. Leaves rustled, and the trees bent low, creaking under the force of the wind. Off to his right, Crane heard a branch crack.

The lightning was spectacular, forking across the sky in vivid paths. As the storm approached them, the thunder increased in volume. Maggie clamped her hands to her ears.

"Does it scare you?" he asked after the noise had rumbled away.

"I hate thunder." She shivered.

He reached for her, then pulled back, afraid she would find his touch as frightening as she found the thunder. Then it boomed again. She turned into his arms, her face against his chest. His nerves echoed the flash and roar of the storm. It was only that she was afraid of the thunder, he warned himself. Her quivering body in his arms had nothing to do with him.

The wind carried a sprinkle of cold raindrops.

"We better get out of this." He eased her toward the tiny shelter. She followed without protest. Each roar of thunder sent a shudder through her, and she clung to him. His heart thundered its own response.

He pulled her inside and eased her to the ground, lowering himself beside her. The willow branches gave off a fresh smell. The enclosure was very small. He closed his eyes. A chill wind tore across the clearing and into the shelter.

"It must have hailed somewhere," he said.

Maggie shivered in his arms. Her teeth rattled. "I'm so cold," she said, chattering.

He threw more wood on the fire. For a moment the logs lay dark and dead, then flared into flames that threw a blanket of warmth toward them. Crane studied the sky. "I believe the storm is moving away."

But despite the passing storm and the increased warmth of the fire, Maggie continued to shiver. "I can't seem to get warm," she said.

"Crawl between the blankets." He pulled her boots off and helped her slide down into the bedroll. "Is that better?"

Her teeth rattling, she said, "I'll get warm in a bit."

He threw more wood on the fire, poured himself another

cup of coffee, then huddled back in the shelter, his knees brushing her shivering form. "You still not warm?"

"No."

He squeezed the cup until his knuckles cracked. The storm had passed, circling to the south of them, so the thunder he heard had to be inside his head. He filled his lungs, then held his breath for a heartbeat. And another. Slowly he let the hot air escape through his open mouth. He eased down beside Maggie, his body matching hers, legs to legs, hips to hips, shoulders to shoulders, separated by the layer of blankets. His hand shaking like leaves in the wind, he lifted the covers.

"Come here—I'll warm you up." He pulled her into his arms.

She came willingly.

His senses flooded with her scent and the feel of her small, lean body. Her hair whispered against his cheek. He closed his eyes. She would never guess how much he ached for them to be truly man and wife. It would take every ounce of his self-control, but he clamped down on his back teeth, promising himself he would not allow his needs and wants to rule his actions.

Slowly her shivering subsided, and she lay soft and relaxed in his arms.

"I've wondered—" She broke off quickly.

"Wondered what?"

She swallowed loudly, then rushed on. "How it would feel to be in your arms like this."

Blood surged through his veins. "I've wondered—" Dare he say anything more? Would she jerk away and retreat to the far corner of the lean-to? He smiled. Not that such a move would put much distance between them. He began again. "I've wondered what your lips would taste like."

She slowly lifted her face. In the golden glow of the fire, he could see her faint smile. His heart threatened to explode, then, accepting her unspoken invitation, he found her lips. It was a gentle, chaste kiss, but he discovered her lips were cool and yielding.

"Soft and sweet," he said. And driving him to want more.

She gave a short laugh. "Warm and cozy."

He knew she was referring to his arms, and he laughed deep in his chest. He felt her straining toward him and took her lips again, this time his kiss deeper, firmer. Her arms stole upward to encircle his neck. He buried his hands in her thick, silky hair.

ᴥ

Crane woke the next morning as pink light gently colored the sky. Maggie lay curled beside him, her hands bunched together under her chin. He filled his senses with her, taking in every detail—the dark fringe of eyelashes across her cheek, her complexion as pretty as the morning sky with the first rays of sunshine.

He'd never seen a sight that gave him more pleasure. He'd never been happier than he was right now, and he breathed deeply, filling each pore with joy.

He took his fill of watching her, then eased himself from under the covers, humming softly as he rekindled the fire and put on a fresh pot of coffee.

"Crane." A little whisper came from some nearby bushes.

"You can come out now, Betsy." He'd known she was there for several minutes.

She hurried to his side, leaning against his shoulder.

"What are you doing up so early?" he asked.

"I missed you."

"I missed you too." He hugged her.

"Was it a good surprise?"

"A very good surprise."

"Then I don't mind missing you for one night."

He smiled. "Do Mr. and Mrs. Strong know you're here?"

She nodded. "Mrs. Strong was feeding the baby. She saw me go."

The coffee boiled, and Crane reached around the child to get a cupful.

"When's Maggie going to wake up?"

Crane shrugged. "I don't know. Do you suppose we should help her?" He had to hold the child back. "Maybe we should do it together." Not for anything would he miss the chance to see Maggie's expression when she first opened her eyes.

He hunkered down at her side, releasing Betsy, who threw herself across Maggie's chest.

"Maggie, wake up." She patted Maggie's cheeks.

Maggie's eyes opened slowly. Crane couldn't breathe as he waited for that moment when she'd see him. She saw Betsy first and groaned. "Who let you in?"

The child leaned back. "Crane did. He said I could wake you up."

"He did, did he?" And her gaze found him.

His heart slammed into his ribs. Half awake, her eyes dark as deep water, she looked so kissable he could hardly stand it. He smiled, not caring that he probably looked like a love-struck fool.

Her cheeks darkened, and her gaze danced away.

"Come on, Maggie—get up." Betsy shook her.

Maggie tried to pull the covers to her chin. Crane caught a glimpse of her bare shoulder, and his mouth dried. Perceiving her difficulty, he caught Betsy in his arms. "Come on, little Miss Betsy. Let's go see how Mrs. Strong is doing."

As they ducked into the open, he whispered over his shoulder, "We'll give you a few minutes."

He and Betsy returned to the main camp. Sally Jane was leaning over the fire, frying bacon. "There you are. Join us for breakfast."

Crane waited for Betsy to settle beside Sally Jane, then he headed back.

"Good morning, Maggie." She sat next to the fire, nursing a cup of coffee. She lifted her gaze. Dark, questioning, and— dare he hope—warm with a just-kissed, just-loved, and mighty-happy-about-it expression.

"Did you have a good night?"

"Slept good." She swirled the coffee around in her cup,

then nodded toward the others.

"How are things over there?"

"Good." He held himself tight, wanting her to say something about last night, wanting her to give him some indication of how she felt. But she only tipped her mug back and forth, studying the dark liquid.

There's time, he warned himself. *Plenty of time. Give her all the time she needs. She's such a young thing.*

The smell of bacon wafted through the trees and made his mouth water. "They said to come for breakfast."

"Guess I'm ready." She went to the shelter and rolled up the bedrolls.

Crane stared after her. Guess that's that. Unfolding arms that were suddenly stiff, he doused the fire and gathered up their few items.

Her arms loaded with bedding, Maggie headed toward the other campsite without looking back. With his heart suddenly cold and heavy, he followed.

Sally Jane looked up, smiled, and ducked her head. Crane wondered what Sally Jane saw that made her look so pleased.

Maggie plunked down and grabbed another cup of coffee. Ted sidled up to her, and she rubbed his hair.

Betsy danced to her side. "We're having bacon and hotcakes. Don't they smell good?" She turned to Sally Jane. "How long 'til it's ready?"

Sally Jane laughed. "Quick as a wink. That is, if Maggie doesn't mind holding Sarah so I can use both hands."

Maggie's smile returned as she reached out and took the baby.

Everything was back to normal, Crane thought later as he threw the saddle over Rebel's back. But things had changed. Even if Maggie seemed set on showing she preferred things to be the same.

He slapped the saddlebags on. Rebel snorted and backed away. "Sorry, old boy. Didn't mean to take it out on you."

If that was the way Maggie wanted it to be, well, so be it.

It took time to become truly man and wife. One night alone under the stars didn't make it signed, sealed, and delivered.

He finished with the horses and paused, resting his hands on the worn, bulky pack. He was balking because she'd pulled at the reins.

He slowly filled his lungs. *Let her set the pace,* he cautioned himself. A colt broken with patience and gentleness was always a better horse than one broken by force. He figured people weren't all that different.

His laugh was more snort as he thought of how Maggie would react if she knew he'd compared her to a horse. Quite sure of her outspoken reaction, he grinned as he led the horses to camp.

Maggie's eyes widened as she stared at him.

He pushed his hat back from his forehead and grinned at her, delighting in the emotions racing across her face. Surprise, wonder, and a flare of something he decided he would take as interest. There was a definite crackle in the air between them.

As he turned to get organized to hit the trail, he hummed tunelessly.

eleven

The sun was hot and the sky so bright it hurt the eyes. The children rode quietly in the wagon. Even the adults made little conversation, the heat sucking at their energy.

Crane watched Maggie out of the corner of his eye. As the morning progressed, she slumped over her chest. He dropped back until he was at her side. "Are you all right?" he murmured, touching her arm.

She jolted up, blinking. "Just hot and tired."

"Maybe we should pull up for the day and wait this heat out." He studied the landscape but saw nothing offering relief.

"No. I'm fine. Besides, how do we know how long it will last?" She glanced at the horizon and shuddered. "Let's keep going and get out of these prairies as quick as we can."

"I'm with you on that," he muttered.

Wally, overhearing part of their conversation, said, "This heat is good growing weather."

Wally could be right for all Crane knew, though he wondered about the lack of rain. Even the thunderstorm last night had produced nothing but a few drops.

By noon the heat was almost unbearable. They pulled to the side of the road and sought the shelter of the wagon.

Baby Sarah fussed.

"Poor wee mite can't take the heat," Wally said, his look forbidding the twins to complain. "Sponge her off, and see if that will help."

Sally Jane did as her husband suggested, then nursed the baby.

"We might as well push on," Wally said. "Sally Jane, you and the baby stay in the wagon, out of the sun."

She climbed in back, and the twins sat on the tailgate.

Crane helped Maggie and the children mount.

"I don't blame Sarah," Betsy whispered as he lifted her up behind Ted. "I'm so hot I want to cry."

"I know, Little Bit. I promise we'll stop if we find some trees or water."

But by late afternoon they had found nothing but a solitary water tower. Crane opened the spout, letting the water cascade over the children. They filled their canteens and watered the horses.

"There must be a dam close by to fill this tower." Wally shielded his eyes against the brittle glare and studied the lay of the land.

"There's a furrow where the pipeline runs." Crane pointed to the north. "But I see nothing but flat prairie."

Wally shrugged. "It could be miles."

"I'll ride over and have a look-see."

Crane rode three miles or more before he found the dam tucked in a deep coulee. Plenty of water was there, but not so much as a twig of a tree. Nothing but scrub buck brush and wild rose bushes loaded with blossoms from white to deep pink. He breathed deeply of the sweetness, then turned back. "We're just as well off here."

Maggie sighed. "Then let's get set up."

Wally pulled the wagon off the trail, angling it to provide a band of shade. He pulled a tarp from the back. "Let's tie this to the side of the wagon. It will help some."

It was too hot for a fire, and with nothing but twigs to burn, they settled for cold meat and biscuits. Crane opened two cans of peaches.

Ted leaned against a wheel, casting a dark look toward the twins. Even Betsy looked fit to go bear hunting.

"You probably won't believe this," Crane began, "But I'd sooner ride in this heat than in a cold rain." He leaned over his knees. "I recall a time we was trailing cows north from down in the States, and it had been raining for five days."

The children faced him.

"Have you ever tried to build a fire in the rain? Or cook a pot of stew with water pouring down into the pot?" He shook his head. " 'T'weren't Cookie's fault, but he was getting the butt of all the complaints."

He glanced around at his listeners. "I want to tell you— you don't want to run into a bunch of cold, wet, hungry cowboys who haven't had decent coffee in days." He chuckled.

"Well Sir, a couple of the boys was really riding Cookie. He threw down his spoon in disgust and muttered, 'Don't see none of yous doing anything but belly achin'.' " And stomped away. But don't you think them old boys had heard the last of it. Cookie waited until they had gone to sleep, then scraped out the pot and dropped a good-sized spoonful of stew on a couple of pairs of boots." Crane grinned at the boys, who sat forward, hanging on his every word.

"Seems Cookie knew some coyotes were slinking about and figured he'd get the last laugh. That night the coyotes found the stew."

Wally started to chuckle.

"What happened?" Ted asked.

"They licked up the stew clean as a whistle, then went for the boots. Well, you can imagine what the boys had to say when they woke up and found their boots half chewed up."

The children stared at him, wide-eyed, their mouths hanging open. Betsy was the first to laugh, then the twins joined in.

"I bet they was real mad," Betsy said.

"Serves them right," Ted muttered. Then a slow grin crossed his face. "I'd like t've seen it."

Crane shrugged. " 'Course they could never be sure it was Cookie's fault."

"You wouldn't have had anything to do with it, would you?" Maggie asked.

He shrugged, barely able to think with her eyes sparkling at him. "I was just a boy. Just the cook's helper."

"Great story," Wally said. "Bet you got a dozen of them."

Crane tore his gaze from Maggie. "You hear a lot of things around a campfire."

"No doubt." Wally turned to the boys. "You two get ready for bed."

Crane nodded at Betsy and Ted. "You too."

After the beds were rolled out, he took the Bible to Maggie. "Might be a good time to read about the flood," he muttered. "All that water sounds good in a place like this."

She choked back a laugh. "You think I should avoid stories of fire and brimstone tonight?"

"Good idea," he murmured.

Her gaze held him, unblinking and dark. And questioning. He was caught in a rushing stream of emotion. What was she wanting? He waited, hoping she would explain.

"You going to read, Maggie?" Betsy's voice rang across the narrow space.

Maggie blinked and lowered her eyes, but not before Crane got the feeling he had disappointed her.

He turned away, crossing his arms over his chest. He was no good at guessing games. She should know that. In fact, one of the things he'd grown to appreciate about her was her directness. Now all of a sudden she had this—this something she wasn't being direct about.

She read the story of Abraham sending his servant to find a wife for his son, Isaac. At the words about Isaac taking Rebekah to his tent and making her his wife, her voice trembled and she hurried to the end.

Crane kept his head lowered, watching from under his eyelashes, barely hearing the last few words. Something about Isaac loving her and being comforted.

He chewed his lip. It hadn't been a tent, only a tiny shelter built from willow branches. But he'd made her well and truly his wife. And it could be comforting if only he knew what she thought.

Sally Jane's voice interrupted his thoughts. "Read again the part where the servant said the Lord had led him."

Maggie found the place and read it again.

Sally Jane sighed. "That's comforting to know God will lead us to the right spot."

Maggie looked up. "I remember a picture Ma had. Probably still hanging up at home. It was of the good shepherd rescuing a lamb that had fallen over a cliff."

Crane could hear the smile in her voice.

"Ma used to say sometimes we don't follow so good and get ourselves into trouble, but even then God doesn't leave us. He comes and finds us. You remember that, Ted?"

"Uh huh."

"I guess that's what He did."

Sally Jane leaned closer. "What do you mean?"

"I'd lost my way. There's no other way to say it. Then God sent Crane, and Crane had this Bible, and I remembered all the things I'd forgotten."

Crane looked at his boots. It wasn't the first time she'd said something that made him feel as if she were calling him some kind of savior. And he wasn't. The idea made him twitch.

Sally Jane spoke again. "God's made you into a special and unique family."

Crane looked around. She was right. They were a family. He and Maggie, Ted and Betsy. A different kind of family but for sure a family. And they'd find themselves a place out West and make a new life. No looking back.

Maggie put away the Bible.

"Let's do like Abraham's servant and ask God to guide us." Sally Jane reached out to take Maggie's and Wally's hands.

Maggie took Crane's hand. A shock raced up his arm. He steadied himself as he reached for Betsy's hand. The children joined hands until they formed a circle, then Wally prayed aloud for God's guidance and protection. A gentle quietness held them after his "Amen." Without speaking, they found their bedrolls.

Crane heard Wally whisper, "Good night, Dear," and kiss his wife.

Betsy shuffled and squirmed, trying to get comfortable.

A light wind came up, carrying the heat of the day, but it stirred the air and eased their discomfort.

Maggie sighed.

Crane ached to ask her what was troubling her, but every word would be overheard. He turned on his side and waited for sleep to come.

❧

The heat still hung over them the next morning. They stopped at noon for another cold meal. Shortly after their noon meal, they saw a town in the distance.

"I've got some things to look after," Wally said as they passed the first scattered buildings.

"A woman's store!" Sally Jane cried. "Could I at least look?"

Wally chuckled. "Look all you like."

"Maggie, I'll get the supplies," Crane offered, "If you want to go with Sally Jane."

The twins and Betsy followed the women; Ted trailed after Crane. He clomped up the steps to the general store, pausing at the doorway to let his eyes adjust to the gloomy interior. The air inside was as hot as outdoors with the added weight of cinnamon, linseed oil, and turpentine smell. Flies buzzed against the grubby window and swarmed across every surface.

Crane stepped up to the counter, took off his hat, and swept the flies away. He reached out and took four cans of peaches and a half dozen cans of beans. He ordered cornmeal and flour, then circled the store, selecting more items he needed.

One corner held a selection of books. He glanced over them and turned away when something else caught his eye. He bent over the display and studied the fine black pen, remembering Maggie's desire to write her father.

He nodded at the man tallying his purchases. "I'll take that." Crane pointed at the pen. "And that." He indicated some ink. "And some paper suitable for letter writing."

A few minutes later he stepped back into the sunshine, pulling his hat low to shade his eyes. Ted followed at his heels.

They crossed to where the wagon and horses were tied. Maggie, Sally Jane, and the children waited in the shade. Wally hurried toward them, then climbed into the back of the wagon with Sally Jane to put away their purchases.

As he half listened to Betsy's chatter, Crane wondered what took them so long to stow a couple of parcels.

When Wally climbed down, he turned to Crane. "I've been asking around. There's lots of land around here. Sally Jane and I agree this is the sort of place where we want to settle. So we'll be stopping here." He cleared his throat and looked from Maggie to Crane. "How about you folks? Why don't you stop here as well?"

Crane met Maggie's gaze, reflecting the blue of the sky. A man could drown in eyes like that. "I think we'll be moving farther west," he murmured.

Sally Jane touched Maggie's shoulder. "I'm sorry. I'll miss you."

"We must at least spend the night together before you move on." Wally called the twins. "We're going to find a spot to camp. This will be the last night we'll all be together."

"Pa, why can't they stay with us?" one twin asked.

"Why don't we go with them?" said the other.

Wally shook his head. "This is as far as we go together."

They camped a stone's throw from town, next to a sluggish creek. Three large trees and a handful of bushes were all that relieved the relentless sun.

Long after the children had fallen asleep, the adults sat drinking coffee and visiting.

Finally Crane pushed to his feet, stretched, and yawned. "I'm for getting some sleep."

"You're right." Wally stood and pulled Sally Jane up beside him. "I'm anxious to see if I can find us a homestead tomorrow."

Sally Jane hesitated. "We'll say our good-byes in the morning." Then she let Wally help her into the wagon.

"Good night all," Wally called before he pulled the canvas over the opening.

Maggie stared into the flames, then sighed heavily as she got to her feet, found her bedroll, and despite the heat, pulled a blanket up to her chin. He drained his cup before he headed for his own bedroll. But sleep didn't come easily. He sensed Maggie was unhappy and put it down to having to part with their newfound friends. He wished he could offer her comfort. His arms ached to hold her, but his mind warned him to caution. She had come to him before, and he figured, if she wanted comfort from him, she would come again on her own.

Next morning they said their good-byes.

"Be sure to write," Wally said. "Let us know where you settle."

Sally Jane and Maggie hugged a long time. When they broke away, Sally Jane dashed tears from her eyes. "If you ever need anything, you let us know."

Maggie stepped away and pulled herself to Liberty's back. She and the children turned around and waved several times, but Crane did not look back.

With every passing mile the heat grew. They rode all day without finding a place to hide from it. Crane's gaze constantly swept the horizon, hoping to find anything that would provide a bit of shade. It was late afternoon, the sun still blasting at them from high in the western sky, before he saw a stand of trees promising relief. It wasn't far from the trail, and he pulled up. "Let's stop here."

The others followed without speaking. The temperature dropped a degree or two as they entered the protection of the trees. The clearing in the center was filled with knee-deep grass. He let his breath out in a whoosh when the horses' hooves sucked at the ground. A step farther and water splashed through the blades of grass.

"Last one in's a rotten egg!" he called.

The children barreled off Ted's horse, whooping.

"Take off your clothes," Maggie ordered.

"Aww," Betsy whined, but Ted had already stripped down to his undershorts and was pushing his way through the grass.

Betsy forgot her annoyance and pulled her dress over her head, tossing it to Maggie.

The children stomped in the water, screeching when it splashed up in their faces. Ted lay down. The water left a circle of flesh on his stomach dry, and he cupped his hands to wet his entire body.

Maggie watched Crane through narrowed eyes, then dropped from her horse. "There's no way I'm passing this up," she muttered and, turning her back to him, pulled her dress off and stood before him in that same skimpy, lace-trimmed garment he'd seen before.

His throat had been parched for some time, waiting for a drink, but the dryness he'd been nursing was nothing compared to the way his tongue felt now.

She jerked off her boots and marched toward the children, her head high.

"Come on, Crane," Betsy called.

"Not now." He turned to set up camp.

Crane watched them as he worked. Maggie spread her arms wide and belly flopped into the water, sending a wide spray across the children, causing Betsy to shriek and Ted to laugh.

Crane swung the saddles off each horse and led the animals to water, leaving them to graze. He trampled down grass and dug a hole for a fire. He didn't care how hot it was; he was going to have coffee tonight.

He tried to ignore sounds of splashing as he gathered wood. Sweat dripped from his chin and soaked his shirt.

Suddenly his nerves zinged. Then three shrieking, wet bodies grabbed him from behind. He staggered and flung them off. Maggie snagged a cup and tore back to the water, where she scooped it full. Crane knew what she intended, but before he could escape, Maggie tossed the water across his chest, soaking his shirt.

"You need to cool off too!" she yelled, grinning widely. "No point in sitting there hot and miserable when you could be having fun."

The children dropped hold of his hands and raced to scoop up water, flicking it in his face.

"I'll show you fun." He lunged for Maggie, but she darted away, laughing.

Shrieking, the children raced after her to stand in the ankle-deep water.

"Think that will save ya?" He tromped after them. The water didn't even come over his boots.

Betsy sat down with a plop. He grabbed her head and pushed her into the puddle, at the same time snagging Ted and flipping him off his feet.

Growling, he headed for Maggie.

She backed away.

He scooped her up in his arms, ignoring how his nerves hummed, and raised her high. "Say uncle," he ordered.

"Never," she sputtered.

"Then you pay." He threatened to drop her. "Uncle?"

She clutched at his arms. "Never."

He uncurled her fingers. "Last chance."

"We'll save you," Ted called.

Two bodies slammed into Crane's legs. He staggered but couldn't regain his balance. He pulled Maggie to his chest, fearing he would fall on her, and landed heavily on his knees, water splashing up.

Maggie scuttled away, turning to face him, her eyes wide. She swallowed hard, then a grin spread across her face. "You're still too dry." She sprayed water on him.

The children tackled him again.

"What's the use?" he muttered and flopped down in the water, rolling over and over until he lay looking up at the bright sky.

The children piled on his chest.

Maggie sat close, her wet garments clinging to her. "Now doesn't that feel better?" she asked. "I bet you're a whole lot cooler."

He swallowed hard. There was no way he was going to tell

her a fire was burning in his heart. He stood up, shaking the water from him, wiping his hands across his hair. "Come on—let's make supper." He emptied the water from his boots before he lit the fire.

Betsy kept up her usual chatter as she knelt beside him, but Crane heard little of what she said. His nerves crackled as Maggie sat nearby, combing the tangles from her hair.

She gasped as the comb caught. "Crane, what's in my hair?" she grumbled.

With his legs feeling as if he'd run a mile, he moved to her side. "Looks like you was rolling in some weeds," he muttered, barely able to speak.

"Can you get it out?"

He opened his mouth, but nothing came out except a strangled croak. He rubbed his palms against his wet trouser legs. His movements stiff and jerky, he plucked at the leaves and grass tangled in her hair. His heart thundered in his ears.

"Got it," he murmured, stepping back so he could breathe.

He cast a desperate look at the puddle of water. He steadied himself and returned to tending the meat.

"We were sure lucky to get so many good things at that town, weren't we, Crane?"

Betsy's thin voice pulled him back to reality. He knew she meant the food and mumbled agreement, suddenly remembering the gift he'd bought for Maggie. In the confusion of parting with the Strongs, he'd forgotten it. He wondered how to present it to Maggie and what she'd think of it.

That evening Maggie read about Jacob's sons and the birth of Joseph. As she explained that it meant Rachel had a baby boy, Betsy started to sob.

"Whatever is the matter?" Maggie asked.

"I miss Baby Sarah," the child sobbed, flinging herself in Maggie's arms. "Don't you?"

"Of course I do. I 'spect we all miss the family."

Betsy put her face close to Maggie's. "Maggie, can we have a baby?"

Maggie gasped.

"Can we, huh?"

Crane tried to choke back his laugh.

"Yeah, maybe, sometime." She threw him a desperate, half-angry look.

Still chuckling deep in his chest, Crane reached out for another cup of coffee. He was about to say something about the fun they could have at that when he saw the tightness around her eyes and bit back the words. He'd almost done what he promised himself he'd never do—say or do something to rush Maggie.

Crane stared into the fire. He'd always considered himself a calm, methodical man who didn't let anything upset his reasoning or set him charging after some fanciful idea. But Maggie had him spinning like a top. It was a lot like getting bucked off a bronc.

Maggie shifted position, and he pulled himself back into control. He went to his saddlebag and pulled out the parcel for Maggie. "Got you somethin'." He handed it to her.

"Me? What would you get me?"

"Guess you'll have to open it and see."

She nodded, but her gaze never left his face.

"Go ahead," he urged.

She ducked her head and untied the strings, then folded back the crackling brown paper.

Crane stood back watching as the paper, pen, and ink lay open on her lap. She didn't say anything. She didn't raise her head. He crossed his arms over his chest.

"Crane, thank you." Her voice was low and thick. "Now I can write Pa." She swallowed hard. "And Sally Jane."

Crane caught the glisten of tears on her cheeks.

He straightened up and took a step toward her.

"No, no," she murmured. "I'm all right. It's so thoughtful of you to get me this." Her eyes shone. "You are such a kind man."

He dropped his arms to his side. Kind? He? Byler Crane? Had anyone ever said that about him before? He opened his mouth to protest, but he couldn't make his lips work. Probably no one would agree with her, but suddenly it didn't matter. Maggie had said he was kind, and that made him feel like something.

He wrapped the feeling around him.

twelve

The feeling lasted all the next day.

Crane found ways of watching Maggie without her being aware of it. It surprised him that she seemed unchanged.

"Will it always be this hot?" Betsy whined.

Crane pulled his thoughts away from Maggie. "Sure hope not."

The day had dawned hot as an oven and had unrelentingly baked them as they plodded down the dusty trail. He'd thought of waiting it out at the campsite, but as Maggie pointed out, "No telling how long this will last. We're just as well off to ride it out. Maybe there'll be relief soon."

But despite the heat his heart was light.

And the countryside had changed. They saw more trees now, and the land rolled along like folds in a length of cloth.

"I'm going to ride over there and have a look around." He rode to the top of a hill and looked west. For a moment he stared, then yelled, "Come up here and see!"

When the others joined him, he pointed west. "See the mountains! The Rockies." They looked like a jagged saw's edge topped with clouds. His heart swelled at the sight. He was finally seeing them.

"They aren't very big," Betsy said.

Crane laughed. "We're miles away yet. Wait until we get to Calgary. I hear they're big as giants."

He stared and stared, unable to get his fill. "Let's have dinner here," he said, never taking his eyes off the horizon.

They didn't stop long before they returned to the trail. In the middle of the afternoon the sky to the east darkened and lightning zigzagged across the sky. Cat, who had been riding in front of Ted, stood, arching her back, her tail like a bottlebrush.

Betsy laughed. "Cat's scared. A scaredy cat."

Maggie frowned, her eyes on the sky. "It looks like a thunderstorm."

"It's a long ways off," Crane said. "Can't hardly hear the thunder."

"Could move this direction."

He grinned at her. "Guess you're right. We best find a place to stop."

She wrinkled her nose. "Not out here. Not in the open." She nodded toward the hills. "Let's find shelter up there."

By the time they climbed the hills, the storm was close enough to make Maggie shudder at every thunderclap.

"These trees will do," Crane called, reining in at the closest bunch.

"Trees aren't safe in lightning." Maggie refused to follow him. "I'm sure we can find something better."

At the look on her face, he decided not to argue. "Let me know when you find what you're looking for." And he let Maggie take the lead.

"There." She pointed. It was a ledge high up the hill.

He nodded. The storm was catching them faster than he'd guessed.

He handed the lead rope of the packhorse to Maggie. "Here—you go on ahead while I get some firewood."

He had his arms full of wood when a flash of lightning almost blinded him. Thunder roared down the side of the hill. With it came a flood of rain, soaking him in a matter of seconds. He heard the frightened whinny of a horse.

Wrapping a piece of canvas around the wood, he secured it to the saddle, then headed for shelter. Water poured down the side of the hill. Rebel struggled to keep his feet under him. Again he heard a horse whinny.

"Come on, Boy. You can do it," Crane urged Rebel upward.

"Maggie!" Ted's yell sent shudders racing down Crane's spine, and he pushed the horse harder. The rain sheeted down so he could hardly see Ted holding Liberty and his own mount. Betsy stood back a few feet, her hair clinging to her head, clutching Cat in her arms.

"Maggie's down there!" Ted yelled, pointing downhill.

Crane's heart leapt to his mouth. "What happened?"

"The packhorse spooked. She tried to hold it. They went down there."

Crane followed the tracks over the edge of the hill. He scrubbed the rain from his eyes and squinted into the murky distance. He could make out the horse, shuddering on the slope.

"Keep back from the edge." He handed Rebel's reins to Ted, then slid down the slope, digging his heels in to slow himself. A flash of lightning allowed him to see through the shroud. Maggie lay face down in the mud. "Maggie!" he yelled, his heart clenching like a fist. "Maggie, answer me."

Water poured down the slope, parting around her body, then cascading past. When she wiggled in the mud, the rain and misery disappeared.

"Give me your hand," he barked.

"No. Take the horse." Her voice was muffled against the ground.

"Forget the horse. Give me your hand."

"The horse," she insisted, turning her head toward him.

They were wasting time arguing. He grabbed the reins, but it was impossible to force the animal up the slippery slope. He skidded down to the trees and tied the animal securely.

"Maggie, I'm coming." But he slid back a foot for every step he made. Digging his hands into the mud, he clawed his way to her side, grabbed her around the waist, and lifted her. His feet slipped. He threw himself sideways, landing on his backside, Maggie in his arms, her icy fingers clutching his shirtfront.

They slid downward. Lightning filled the sky. Moaning, Maggie buried her face against his chest as the thunder echoed and reechoed across the hill. They ground to a halt a few feet from the horse.

Maggie was muddy from head to toe, drenched like a little rat. He didn't want to leave her, but he had to go back for Ted and Betsy. He gently removed her from his lap and set her on the ground. "Wait here while I get the children."

She huddled there, spitting mud from her mouth.

Ignoring the pain under his rib cage, he jerked to his feet and found a grassy spot that gave him better traction. He crawled back to the spot where he'd left the children. Betsy threw herself at him, clinging to his muddy knees. "I fot we was lost."

"We have to go to Maggie," Crane said. "I'll take the horses. Ted, you and Betsy stay close."

Ted nodded, swallowing hard.

"Put Cat down," he told Betsy. "She'll have to follow on her own."

Betsy did as he said. Cat pranced from paw to paw but stayed at their side.

"Now hang on tight," he said, knotting the reins in his fist and taking a child in each hand. Betsy shrieked as her feet went out from under her, then they skidded down to the trees.

Water running down her neck, Maggie sat huddled in a heap just as he had left her. Betsy flung herself at her, but Maggie only shuddered.

Ted stood over the pair. "Maggie?"

But Maggie only tightened her arms around her knees.

Crane looked at the miserable trio. The rain fell in buckets. He shook his head, wiping water from his eyes. A fire was impossible, and there wasn't a dry inch where they could find shelter. He pulled a piece of canvas from the pack, keeping it folded against his body as he returned to the others. He edged his legs between Ted and Maggie and pulled Betsy to his lap, then flipped the canvas open covering Maggie, Ted, and Betsy. The rain ran off the canvas washing down his back. Lightning blinded him, accompanied by a roar of thunder. The smell of gunpowder filled the air. Maggie shuddered and moaned while Betsy clawed at his chest and Ted pressed into his side.

"We're safe," he murmured.

Cat pushed her nose under a corner and crawled into Ted's lap.

At that moment Maggie moaned, pushed aside the canvas, and dashed away.

"Maggie?" Crane called, but she didn't answer. He strained to hear and thought he caught the sound of someone being sick.

She returned and crawled back under the protection.

"You all right?" he asked.

She shuddered. "Think I swallowed some mud. My stomach doesn't like it."

He pulled her under his arm, wrapping the canvas as tightly as possible around her shivering shoulders, but again Maggie pushed away and fled for the trees. He lost count of the number of times she made the trip. He didn't know how long they sat huddled in the rain. It seemed like hours. Finally the rain slowed to a drizzle, then quit. It was so dark he couldn't make out the horses tied a few feet away.

"I'm going to see if I can get a fire going." He found Rebel and untied the bundle of wood he'd gathered earlier. He spaded the wet sod away to form a circle of bare ground and carefully arranged the wood. It took several tries before he got the fire started.

Steam rose from the wet ground. Warmth curled toward the others, and slowly the canvas lowered.

Crane couldn't remember when he'd seen a sorrier-looking bunch—Ted pale, his hair plastered to his head; Betsy's eyes round as saucers, her hair hanging in dark tangles, mud clinging to her face and hands.

Crane's chest tightened. Maggie looked the worst, her face streaked, her clothing covered with mud, grass, and leaves. But it was the pinched look around her eyes and the tightness of her lips that made Crane clench his teeth. She lurched to her feet and dashed into the stand of trees.

Crane stared after her before he turned his attention to Betsy, stripping her down to her undergarments, rubbing her down with a towel, removing mud and water in one operation, then finding her dry garments.

Maggie returned as he finished, and he said to the child, "Stand here and stay warm while I take care of Ted."

When both children were cleaned and dried as best he could, he spread the canvas on the ground and, finding a dry blanket in the pack, had them lie down. Before he was finished, Maggie had disappeared into the trees again, clutching her belly. He set water to boil and waited for her to return.

The children fell asleep. Cat sat by the fire cleaning her fur. Crane stared into the trees. Maggie had been gone a mighty long time. He wanted to go to her but was afraid he'd embarrass her. He washed the worst of the mud off himself and put on a dry shirt, then hooked the wet blankets and clothing over branches near the fire.

Still Maggie hadn't returned. He called her name. Only the crack of the logs in the fire and the drip of water from the leaves answered him. He grabbed a piece of wood from the fire, a flickering circle of light landing ahead of him.

"Maggie," he called, following her tracks. "Maggie, where are you?"

The trees rained on him, soaking his shirt again, but he merely shook his head and pushed on. "Maggie." *What could have happened to her?*

He saw her curled up on the wet ground and sprang to her side.

"Maggie." But she didn't answer. He touched a trembling hand to her shoulder.

She moaned but didn't open her eyes. He scooped her into his arms and hurried back to the fire. His heart thudding thickly, he snagged one of the damp blankets, throwing it on the ground. Gently he laid her on it. She curled into a ball.

She wouldn't thank him for moving her about, but he couldn't leave her in her wet clothing. His fingers clumsy, he unbuttoned her dress and pulled it off. It was soiled with mud and sickness. Her undergarment was soiled as well, and he struggled to remove it. Tenderly he sponged her face, her hands, her trembling body.

She moaned and drew her knees to her belly. He wrapped a towel around her, holding her in his arms, trying to warm her with his body, trying to calm the shudders shaking her small frame. Warmth slowly seeped into her. Still he held her.

It had been some time since her body had erupted. He decided the worst of the stomach upset was over. His arms cramped. His back ached. Pins and needles raced up and down his legs, but he did not lay her down.

Although he sat as still as a rock, his mind raced. "Maggie mine, do you have any idea how much I love you?" he murmured. "I can't stand to see you suffer like this. I wish it was me instead."

He would do anything for her. The knowledge of his love seared through his body. He'd loved her since she faced Bull. He loved the way she said what she thought, the way she tended the children so gently, the way she teased. He loved everything about her. If only he could make her see that.

He remembered when she had asked about the future. He knew she'd been seeking assurances from him, and he had refused to give them. He stared at the fire without blinking.

Sure, he excused himself. He didn't believe in making promises he couldn't be sure of keeping, but it wouldn't have hurt him to give her something to hang on to.

He vowed he would find a way of telling her how much she had come to mean to him.

Not until he felt her body relax, not until her legs no longer pulled up to her midsection, did he carefully lower her next to the children.

He couldn't bring himself to dig through her clothes, so he pulled one of his shirts from the saddlebags and eased her arms into the sleeves. A pulse thudded in his temple as he fastened the buttons down the front.

Her head lolled in exhaustion. He covered her warmly, then leaned against the nearest tree, watching her sleep.

To the east the sky was already turning gray. He turned his face upward. *God, it's been a long time, but here I am. I guess I never quit believing in You. But it's like Maggie says—I got lost somewhere.*

More of Maggie's words filled his brain—like how God sent His Son, Jesus, so he, Byler Crane, could have his sins forgiven. And how it was as easy as accepting a gift. Just like that little boy who took the coin from the preacher man.

So here I am, God. Ready to accept that gift. Ready to trust You. He'd never been good at trusting, but this time it was easy. He remembered when home had meant feeling good. That same feeling settled into the edges of his heart. He filled his lungs slowly before he continued.

Maggie's always saying how You're ready to help us anytime, so I could sure use some help right about now. Not for myself, you understand. But for Maggie.

≈

Crane woke with a beam of sun in his face and jerked upright. Everyone else still slept. Maggie, dark shadows under her eyes, moaned.

He tried to decide what was best to do. Only one canteen of water was left. Either he would have to go and find water, or they would have to move camp closer to water. But Maggie and the children were still exhausted. Maggie wouldn't be strong enough to ride today.

They had the added threat of another storm. The idea of being caught in another like last night was enough to make him shudder.

He eased to his feet and crept away to a spot where he could study the surrounding land. For a long time he gazed at the scene before him. The mountains weren't visible today, hidden in the misty horizon. To the north he could see a heavy shower, then a spear of sun broke through and painted a rainbow across the sky. He could hear the distant wail of a train.

He returned to camp and quietly saddled Rebel.

"Where are you going?" Maggie's weak voice spun him

around. She watched him with shadowed eyes.

His throat tightened. "How are you feeling?"

"Like a wet dishrag." Her voice cracked, and he sprang to get her a drink.

Her hands shook as she took the cup, and he steadied it, wrapping his fingers over her cold ones.

She lay back, panting.

He grabbed one of the dry blankets and wrapped it about her.

"Were you going someplace?" She sounded weary.

"We need water." He rubbed his neck. How could he leave her? Yet they had to have water.

"How far do you have to go?"

He shrugged. "Can't say for sure."

She tried to sit up. "It might storm again."

"Lay down and keep covered."

She shook his hands off and pushed the covers down. "I don't want to spend another night here."

Both children wakened and listened to the exchange.

"Crane, it was so awful," Betsy whispered. "I was so scared, but I kept thinking of that picture Maggie told us about." She touched Maggie's face. "You know. The one where Jesus reached down and helped the lost lamb."

She shuddered. "I know He helped us, but I don't want to stay here."

Ted nodded.

"I suppose it's best if we stay together." Crane sighed. "On one condition." He gave Maggie his fiercest look. "You don't do anything."

Her eyes narrowed, and he feared she was going to argue, but she sighed deeply and flopped down. "I don't think I'll mind taking things easy for a bit."

"Betsy, you gather up all the stuff hanging on the trees. Ted, you help with the horses."

The children scampered to do his bidding. He couldn't tear himself away from the look Maggie gave him. How much did she remember from last night? Had she heard his confession of love? He waited, hoping she would somehow let him know, but instead she sighed and turned away.

"I know I'm causing you a lot of trouble—" Her voice trailed off.

Laughing, he stood to his feet. "This is nothing." He wanted to make light of it, tell her a story about trying to corral some wild cows, somehow convince her he'd handled much worse situations, but he felt hollow inside. He knew he'd never faced anything in his life that made his nerves shake the way they did as he thought of making Maggie ride in her weakened condition.

As soon as they were ready, he lifted her to the saddle. She gripped the saddlehorn so hard her knuckles turned white.

"Are you sure you're up to this?"

She gritted her teeth. "I can do anything I make up my mind to do."

"No doubt," he muttered, leading them down the hill.

By the time they reached the bottom, Maggie's lips had a strained white ring around them. It wasn't a hot day; yet beads of sweat stood out on her forehead. He opened his mouth to say something, but she glared at him and muttered, "I'm fine."

He turned away mumbling, "Of course you are. And I'm the king's brother."

"What'd you say, Crane?" Betsy called.

"Nothin'. Just thinkin' out loud."

"I'm hungry."

"I know." She'd done well to be so patient. "Just a bit longer."

A glance over his shoulder at Maggie clinging bravely to the saddle sent a squeezing tightness around his ribs.

A bunch of trees came in sight. He glimpsed a reflection of a stream through the trees and heaved a sigh. "We'll set up camp here."

He soon had a fire going, and while Ted tended a pot of oatmeal, he built a shelter and carried Maggie to it. By the time he'd tugged her boots off and pulled the covers around her shoulders, she was asleep.

"Is she all right?" Ted asked, his face creased with worry.

"I 'spect so. Just a little weak from being sick." He said the words with a lot more conviction than he felt. "We'll stay here until she feels stronger."

Satisfied with his answer, the children played with Cat.

Maggie slept the rest of the afternoon and into the next day. Crane stayed close by, trying to hide his worry from the children. He sat nursing a coffee, staring at the flickering flames, when he heard her clear her throat.

"Got any more of that?" She nodded toward his cup.

He leapt to his feet and took her some coffee. "You feeling better?"

She drank several swallows before she answered. "Better'n what?"

He laughed. "Guess you must be."

"You going to stand there gawking or get me something to eat?"

He laughed again. "What would Madame like?" He was so relieved to see her awake, he would have gone bear hunting if she'd asked.

"Food would be good," she muttered.

His shout of laughter brought the children running.

He cooked her oatmeal, figuring it would be easy on her stomach. By the time she finished, her eyelids were closing. He eased her back to the bed. He could barely breathe. *Thank You, God, for her strength. And her beauty.* He sat there a long time.

&

When the coffee boiled the next morning, she rolled over so she could watch the fire. "I'm feeling much better today."

"I'm glad." He sat beside her.

"I mean we should be moving along today."

He stared at her. He knew better than to argue when she had that look, but he had no intention of dragging her across the country, wilting like a flower in the sun.

"I mean it," she mumbled. "What's the point in sitting here staring at the sky day after day?"

"The point," he ground out the words, "Is in letting you get your strength back."

"I think I'm fit to be the best judge of that."

"You'd think so."

She didn't blink before his glare. "I think I am." She smiled.

Maggie could have asked for anything at that moment. He clamped his mouth shut and tried to think of something halfway intelligent to say. And failed.

She continued to smile at him as she called, "Ted, Betsy, up and at it. We're heading out as soon as we're ready."

Betsy erupted from her blankets. "Good. I'm tired of waiting around. What's for breakfast?"

Ted emerged more slowly. "I'll go get the horses."

Crane had lost the battle. He prepared to leave, but his thoughts troubled him. How was he going to tell Maggie how he felt about her?

❧

For days, Maggie was exhausted after a few hours in the saddle, and they stopped early; but as she said, they were making progress slowly.

Crane wished he could likewise feel he was making progress with Maggie, but with each passing day, they slipped back more and more into the roles they had before the storm. He sighed. It wasn't that he didn't enjoy the way they had been; he simply wanted more.

He practiced how he would tell her he'd changed, but the time never seemed right. And it grew more and more difficult to find the words.

Days later, with the sun glistening off the Rockies, they rode down the streets of Calgary. The children couldn't stop staring at the elaborate sandstone buildings, some three stories tall.

Crane had heard about the fire of '86 that had taken out a

large part of the town. After that the town fathers had encouraged the use of sandstone for building.

He saw a sign that said "Attorneys at Law" and marked the spot in his mind.

Maggie swayed in the saddle. They needed to find a place soon.

He reined in at the general store and hurried inside. "I'm looking for some temporary quarters."

The pot-bellied man eyed him up and down. "Rooms for rent at any of the hotels." Crane shook his head. "Don't want a room. I need a place my wife can rest for a few days." He jerked his head toward the door.

The man shuffled over to peer out the window. "That your family?"

"Yup."

"I see what you mean. Your wife looks done in."

"She's been sick."

Bushy eyebrows jerked up. "She still sick?"

Crane shook his head. "Just tired of riding."

The man hesitated, then gave a brisk nod. "I don't usually do this, but I have a house on the edge of town that's empty. You're welcome to it as long as you need."

" 'Preciate that."

They made arrangements, and Crane bought supplies. Then he led the tired trio to the house.

"We'll be staying here for now." He took in the upturned chairs, the mattresses rolled up on the two sets of bunks. It was dirty, but nothing that couldn't be swept up. "It'll do."

He set one chair upright and pushed Maggie to it. "You sit," he ordered, "while we get things cleaned up."

She nodded.

He figured it was a good measure of how poorly she felt that she put up no argument.

"Ted, there's wood out back. Let's get a fire going and heat some water. Betsy, get the broom I bought."

He cleaned the beds first, then unrolled some bedding and

lay Maggie down. She was as limp as a rag in his arms. She curled on her side, bunched her hands at her chin, and slept. The dark circles under her eyes troubled him.

Hours later, with the children's help, he'd gotten rid of the cobwebs and crud. He brought in the saddles and packs. Ted pumped water into the trough at the back for the horses as Crane prepared supper.

Maggie stirred long enough to eat a few mouthfuls of stew, then fell asleep again.

"Maggie's sure tired a lot." Betsy's voice was thin with worry.

"She just needs some rest," Crane assured the child, praying he was right.

"She was pretty sick after the storm, wasn't she?" Ted asked.

"Guess she got some dirty water in her stomach."

"She's going to be all right, isn't she?" Ted asked as he perched on the edge of his chair.

"I'm pretty sure she is." Crane chuckled. " 'Spect she'd skin us alive if she could hear us talking."

Ted smiled. " 'Spect you're right."

Betsy leaned against Crane. "Nobody's read to us for days."

He wrapped his arm around her. "I do believe you're right. Do you know what?"

She shook her head.

"I bet I could read you a story."

She turned her big brown gaze to him. "For sure?"

"Yup. I believe I could. As soon as you're ready for bed."

She didn't have to be told twice. "Can I sleep here?" She pointed to the other lower bunk and, at Crane's nod, spread her bedroll. "Will we have a house as nice as this when we get where we're going?"

"Yup. Maybe even nicer."

Ted looked thoughtful. "We just about there?"

"Yup."

He sighed. "Good."

Crane studied the boy. He'd never complained or shown

any sign of being tired. Crane shook his head. If the truth be told, he guessed he was about ready to settle down too.

Betsy handed him the Bible. In the far corners of his mind, he remembered something his ma had read and found it.

" 'The Lord is my shepherd. I shall not want.' "

He read the whole psalm, then closed the book. The room was quiet as Crane searched for the words he wanted to say.

"You know, everything Maggie's been telling us about God is true. I think I always knew it, but somehow I figured I didn't need it. But it's like she says, even when we forget about God and get lost, He finds us and helps us back."

He thought of how easy it was to come back. "I remember my own ma saying how God loved us so much He sent Jesus, His Son, to be the way back to God." Maybe Ma was like Maggie; she got so lost in her hurt and anger after Pa left that she forgot about God's love and only remembered it just before she died. That was what she'd tried to tell him. That was why she was so all-fired set he take the Bible.

"This story we read about the shepherd," he patted the Bible, "It's a story that tells us how He leads us and guides us and takes care of us."

Betsy's muffled voice came from her bunk. "Is He taking care of Maggie right now?"

"I'm sure He is, but it doesn't hurt to ask Him."

All was quiet.

"You mean pray, don't you?" Ted asked.

"Yup."

"I don't know how to pray," Ted whispered. "All I know how to do is cuss."

His words startled Crane. Apart from the first day or two, he'd never heard the boy cuss.

"I do it inside me."

Crane took a deep breath, wishing he was better at finding words. "I 'spect praying is as simple as talking to God."

"Crane." It was Betsy. "You pray."

He almost choked. But he couldn't refuse. He swallowed

hard. "God," he began, "thank You for finding us when we're lost. Now we're needing a shepherd to help us and lead us. And most of all we need You to make Maggie better." He fell silent. Suddenly he had so many things he wanted to say, but he couldn't find the words.

"Now I know she'll be fine." Betsy's voice was full of confidence, and she shuffled around in bed, getting comfortable. "Good night, Crane," she called. " 'Night, Ted."

Long after the children had settled, Crane sat up. Somehow, he promised himself, before they left this place, he would find a way of telling Maggie he loved her. His heart lurched as he remembered their agreement—no romance, just partners. What if she preferred to keep it that way?

He pressed his forehead to his palms. If she did, then he would accept it, living his love out quietly, but he could not let it go on without telling her.

If only he was better with his words.

&

They stayed in the little house several days. Crane waited and watched for a chance to tell Maggie how he felt, but the chance never seemed to come. The children were always close by, or Maggie was tired, though he was pleased to see her gaining strength every day.

He'd made several trips downtown, visiting the lawyer, asking where the best land was, and purchasing supplies and equipment to set up a new place. Returning from one of his trips, he paused to look at the house. Smoke snaked up the chimney. He smelled savory meat and fresh bread.

He opened the door. Maggie sat peeling potatoes.

"Crane! Crane! You're back!" Betsy wrapped herself around his legs.

He scooped her up and tossed her high.

She giggled. "Do it again."

He tossed her up again, then tucked her under his arm like a sack of potatoes.

Ted got up from the floor where he'd been playing with

Cat. "I took care of all the chores you gave me."

"Good boy." He ruffled the boy's hair.

He crossed to the table. "And how about you, Maggie? What have you been doing with yourself?"

She glanced up. "Nothing much." She ducked her head again but not before Crane caught the sheen of unshed tears.

He waited, but she kept her head down. He set Betsy on her feet. "Ted." He didn't take his focus off Maggie. "Take Betsy outside for a bit." He waited for the door to close behind them.

Still she didn't lift her head, and the knife in her hand remained idle. He knelt, trying to see her eyes, but she pressed her chin down.

"Maggie." His throat tightened. He swallowed hard and tried again. "Maggie. What's the matter?"

She shook her head.

He tipped her chin up. Tears trailed down each cheek. "Are you sick?"

Again she shook her head.

He jiggled her chin until she lifted her glistening eyes.

"You've got to tell me what's wrong."

She took a long, trembling breath. "I've ruined it all, haven't I?"

He blinked. What on earth was she talking about? He glanced around the room half expecting to see a torn blanket or a failed cake, but he saw nothing. He wanted nothing more than to kiss away the tears and hold her tight. Instead he asked, "What are you talking about?"

"First the children. Then insisting we go up to the hill." She sobbed once, then continued. "Now on top of it all, after agreeing our marriage was going to be businesslike, I've gone and fallen in love with you." Her words ended in a wail.

She pulled away and hid her face. "I'm sorry," she whispered. "I never meant to say that."

His heart thudded against his ribs as if it'd been shot from a cannon. He couldn't move. "Are you crying because you love me?"

Her head jerked up. "No, of course not. I'm crying because I'm so tired of keeping it a secret."

He laughed low in his throat.

She blinked and narrowed her eyes. "Why are you laughing?"

"Because, my dear sweet Maggie, I love you and have been trying to find a way to tell you and wondering if you'd be angry at me." He chuckled and leaned forward, resting his forearms across her knees. "Doesn't it strike you as the least bit funny that we both felt the same way?"

She smiled. "Guess you were as foolish as me."

"Foolish and crazy," he agreed. "Crazy in love with you, Maggie mine."

Her cheeks turned rosy. "I can't believe it."

He caught her chin and waited for her gaze to stop its restless darting about. When it did, he almost fell apart at the love he saw.

"When did you first know?" she whispered.

"I admitted it when you slid down that muddy slope and got so sick." He shuddered. "You had me worried, I'll say." He chased away that dark moment. "But I think I fell in love the day you stood up to Bull." He grinned. "Knew then I'd found me a real woman."

"A real troublemaker, you mean," she muttered.

"Just someone willing to help another even if it isn't easy." He trailed his finger along her jawline. He wanted to run a path of kisses along the same path, but first he had to know. "When did you fall in love with me?"

Her cheeks glowed. Her eyes were dark and shiny.

He could feel his heart pulsing in his throat at the way she looked at him.

"That night."

His breath exploded from him. He knew she meant the night they'd shared the little willow shelter. He wanted to laugh and yell and dance around the room. Perhaps he would later, but there was something he wanted even more than that. He leaned closer but found he didn't have to lean very far, for she met him halfway.

He found her lips. At the same time he found the love he'd wanted all his life.

Later, after the children were put to bed, Maggie climbed into her bunk and patted the space beside her.

Grinning, he crawled under the covers and took her in his arms. "I love you, Maggie mine."

She laughed against his chest. "And I love you, Byler Crane."

A warm feeling filled him. Except for his ma, no one had called him Byler since he was a youngster.

She tapped his chest with one finger. "We've had some good experiences on this journey."

"And a few bad ones." But lying with her in his arms, he had a hard time remembering them.

"And I've found God again."

"Me too."

She squeezed him, making it difficult for him to keep his thoughts on the conversation. "And now it's time to finish our journey and build ourselves a new home."

He was quiet a moment, trying to find the words he wanted. "Our journey won't be over," he said. "It will be only starting."

"You're right."

He half sat. "I almost forgot."

She pulled him down again. "I'm sure it will wait until morning."

He laughed. "It will. It's only another part of the beginning of our journey together."

"Umm. What?"

"I knew you wouldn't be able to let it go." He chuckled.

"I can too." She snuggled close.

He pressed his face into her hair, breathing in the scent of her, and waited.

"I think maybe I want to know." Her voice was muffled against his chest.

He laughed, pleased with his knowledge of her. Then he

murmured, "I went to see a lawyer here. To find out about the children. He says you can apply for guardianship of Ted and name me as joint guardian, or if your pa will relinquish his rights, we can adopt him."

He felt her waiting stillness. "That's up to you. He'll act on your behalf if you like.

"I told him all we know about Betsy, and he sent out some letters. He says there shouldn't be any problem with us adopting her."

"I'm glad. It's the beginning for all of us."

"Tomorrow, if you're feeling up to it, we'll head north. I hear there's fine land available up there."

"I'm up to it." Before he found her lips again, he breathed a silent prayer. *Thank You, God, for this family. For the children. But especially for Maggie, my bride.*

····Heartsong····

Presents

Romance
on the Rails

*T*rain travel promises speed, convenience, and adventure for Americans of the nineteenth century. But four young women are carrying excess baggage on their journeys. Uprooted from secure homes and forced to reexamine their positions in life, can any of them entertain *Romance on the Rails?*

Will the swaying of the coach and the clickety-clack of the train wheels lull these young women into a dream world of false romance? Or will God show them a love as strong as the steel rails on which they ride?

paperback, 352 pages, 5 ³⁄₁₆" x 8"

❤ ❤ ❤ ❤ ❤ ❤ ❤ ❤ ❤ ❤ ❤ ❤ ❤ ❤ ❤ ❤ ❤ ❤

❤ ❤ ❤ ❤ ❤ ❤ ❤ ❤ ❤ ❤ ❤ ❤ ❤ ❤ ❤ ❤ ❤ ❤

A Letter To Our Readers

Dear Reader:

In order that we might better contribute to your reading enjoyment, we would appreciate your taking a few minutes to respond to the following questions. We welcome your comments and read each form and letter we receive. When completed, please return to the following:

Rebecca Germany, Fiction Editor
Heartsong Presents
PO Box 719
Uhrichsville, Ohio 44683

1. Did you enjoy reading *Crane's Bride* by Linda Ford?
   ☐ Very much! I would like to see more books
      by this author!
   ☐ Moderately. I would have enjoyed it more if

   _____

   _____

   _____

2. Are you a member of **Heartsong Presents**? Yes ☐ No ☐
   If no, where did you purchase this book?_____

   _____

3. How would you rate, on a scale from 1 (poor) to 5 (superior),
   the cover design?_____

4. On a scale from 1 (poor) to 10 (superior), please rate the
   following elements.

   _____ Heroine   _____ Plot

   _____ Hero   _____ Inspirational theme

   _____ Setting   _____ Secondary characters

5. These characters were special because_____

_____

_____

6. How has this book inspired your life?_____

_____

_____

7. What settings would you like to see covered in future **Heartsong Presents** books?_____

_____

_____

8. What are some inspirational themes you would like to see treated in future books?_____

_____

_____

9. Would you be interested in reading other **Heartsong Presents** titles?   Yes ❏   No ❏

10. Please check your age range:
    ❏ Under 18   ❏ 18-24   ❏ 25-34
    ❏ 35-45   ❏ 46-55   ❏ Over 55

Name _____

Occupation _____

Address _____

City _____ State _____ Zip _____

Email _____